# Escapades of Love

Hilary Forde

**This book is dedicated to the young life of**

**Chris Edwards**

1964 - 2013

# A Snowdrop

Hope is such a tender fragile flower
When all seems lost we nurture every hour
Until the frost of winter covers all
And the petals wither fade to fall
Yet faith's the rising of the sun
Upon the blossom yet to come

Trust is such a blooded thorn held clasp
Yet to the rose we're drawn to clasp
When left alone the beauty lasts
Upon the moments as they pass
As faith's the rising of the sun
Upon the blossom yet to come

Truth is change as Bluebells gently ring
Bring memories of how it's always been
I hear them softly on the wind
As spring eternal calls again
And love's a Snowdrop in the dawn
That grows for you and I as one
And faith's the rising of the sun
Upon the blossoms yet to come

By Chris Edwards

First published in Great Britain in 2013 by
Majesteeq Press (UK)

This paperback edition published in 2013



A CIP catalogue record for this book is available from the British Library.

978-0-9574470-2-8

# FORTHCOMING

## DOWN MARKET

A Novelette.

Jan had a pipe dream of running a market stall selling her craft work, homemade jams and cakes, but local dogs and young children had different ideas when bad weather befell the day causing chaos; this together with a rather unpleasant woman whose aim was to sabotage the whole thing. All wrapped up in a helping of court, prison sentence, and a good dose of love.

## A TRIP TO SOUTH AFRICA

A Novella.

Meg had the trip of her lifetime offered to her as a volunteer in South Africa to help with the building of a school. Dubious about leaving her son and husband for two months, but thrilled at the prospect. That was until her plane landed at the airport...

# THE SECRETS OF THE MANOR

A Book

Georgina and her sister Lucinda were orphans raised by their loving grandparents Lord and Lady Altringham in their idyllic, historical Manor House. Lucinda married and emigrated to New Zealand. However, Georgina's life took a very different path.

Facing tragedy and challenges; Georgina uncovers The Manor's secrets leading to mystery, intrigue and romance...

## Contents

# About the Author

Hilary Forde was born in Berkhamsted, Hertfordshire. A good few years ago, when owner of a nightclub in Wimbledon that was a "Country Music" hot spot, she wrote regularly for various music magazines. She also wrote sleeve notes for artist's albums. Then some years ago she moved on to broadcasting on a hospital radio station's, and here she edited and compiled the stations "Patients Magazine" for a number of years.

In her younger days she competed and taught Ballroom dancing.

Hilary is married with three children all of whom have fledged. It is through the encouragement of these children she has taken up writing again, but this time in the form of books. She has always been an avid reader.

Acknowledgements

My first thanks must go to my lovely family. They have always inspired me.

Many thanks go to the people who have encouraged and helped me; they are my many friends whose support has been invaluable. Thanks too for my tutor Denise Briden; a person who fills me with inspiration along with my dear friends at college particularly Carol.

I'm indebted to my husband and thank him who has been of constant help especially with my computer when it throws a wobbly; or me who can also throw the odd one.

Lastly, to my talented granddaughter Charlotte, who has so beautifully designed my book cover.  A great big THANKS.

**Hilary Forde**

# The Forgotten Present

The big night is a week away. Only a week till Amber's birthday party! Amber Lacey, my very best friend will be twenty-five. The big thing about the party is that HE is going to be there. Amber has assured me. I, Fran Parsons, must look better than my best; I've really got to stun him. I hugged myself in glee. Right. Book a hair appointment, and also get to the beauty salon for waxing and a facial. Then onto the nail bar for my talons. After that, I'll hit Monsoon or Coast, or maybe Karen Millen. Oh my God! A week won't be long enough to do everything. I'll question Amber about him. That wonderful, handsome guy Matt Granger.

Amber's phone rang and rang; I was at the point of hanging up when a breathless voice answered.

'Hi Amber. It's me Fran. Will you do me a favour? Give me some info on Matt Granger. Is he married or involved? Does he live near? Please don't tell me he's gay.'

'Ok, ok. Steady on. He's free, on the market, and lives about six or seven miles away. He's an acquaintance of my husband. He has a good position at Browns, the IT Company. He was in a full-on relationship until about six months ago. Will that do?'

I'm conscious of grinning from ear to ear at that lovely news.

'Thanks, you're a pal.'

'That's all right. I'll see whether Tony can put in a good word for you. Bye. See you at the party and good luck.'

My next job must be to find an appropriate gift for Amber. Yes! I'll get her the gorgeous faux fur wrap I saw in that new boutique; it's her to a 'T'.

The night of the party has arrived. I feel good. The stylist has put my hair in a chignon, which suits me much better than I expected. My dream of a dress in white satin leaves one shoulder bare, with a trim of deep pink lilies trailing from the other shoulder, crossing the front of the bodice, and wrapping round across the back ending at the hem, just above my knee. My jewellery is simple: expensive Swarovski crystal teardrop earrings with matching necklace, teamed with the decoration the stylist put in the top of my chignon. The finishing touch is the solitaire ring, bequeathed by my Grandmother. I am wearing killer-heels, matching the pink of the lilies. I twist and turn in front of my mirror. Wow! Although I say it myself I feel, and am certain, I look stunning. Mr. Matt Granger, HERE I COME!

When Amber opened the door she took a step back.

'Fran, you look wonderful; get in there and knock him dead!'

With a lift of my chin, I do just that. Matt spotted me at once, he came over to me and introduced himself while leading me over to the bar for a drink, and boy do we talk. We hit the dance floor where I feel wonderful in his arms. This is where I belong. It is such a heady evening. I feel so light-headed that I am just going with the flow; whatever Matt suggests I submit to as I float along.

Suddenly I feel strange; we're moving without walking. I realise we're in a car, as lethargy takes over, and insensible darkness swamps my dreams. Sitting up slowly, my head won't stop spinning. Why does it hurt so much? Where are my lovely dress and shoes? Whose bed am I on? The darting pain behind my eyes stabs at my very consciousness as, once again, sleep overwhelms me.

Groggily I awaken. '*What time is it?*' I groan as I look for a clock, but there isn't one. Stumbling around in the darkness it's clear to see it is not a proper room, let alone a bedroom. Gradually Matt's face emerges in my mind as the last person I saw. Then with complete horror I discover the door is locked, there is no window, my evening purse is missing and so are my expensive pieces of jewellery. The reality dawns on me; I've been abducted, robbed! My debit and credit cards were all in my purse; wherever that is now and my jewellery, including the solitaire and my platinum watch has gone too, and very obviously, so has my mobile phone.

My mind clears slowly as I contemplate my predicament. I gather whoever my abductor is, I suspect Matt, has discovered how wealthy my parents are. I could be worth money, my own personal money or that of my parents. Flopping down on the so-called bed, I curl up and sob, wishing I could awaken from this nightmare. How on earth am I going to get away? Surely when my parents discover I have not come home they will report my disappearance. Perhaps they'll contact Amber. She'll tell them I left the party with that rat of a so-called man, Matt. I just don't know what will become of me. Obviously someone will release me; they can't leave me to rot to death.

Day has turned into night again; I need some food and water. What have I done to deserve this? I don't treat people badly, and Matt appeared to enjoy my company. I thought we were having a good time. I know I have money, as do my parents. Is it for that? I wonder, because I haven't been physically assaulted in any way. I doze again...

Morning? It must be. Lack of food and water has left me weakened, and confused. This must be the end of me. I curl up, ready to die, but my mind won't stop working. Terrifyingly, death beckons, but I'm not ready. I have so much to live for, so much to do with my life. Oh please God, help me!

More hours pass in drugged slumber...

Stiffly I rouse myself, growing aware of unfamiliar snuffling noises, and strange voices; they're coming from behind the door but my fuzzy mind convinces me that I'm dreaming. Turning over, I try to retreat into the sanctuary of sleep. The sounds seem to fade, thank goodness. Sleep. I can submerge myself in the forgetfulness of sleep. Muffled sounds like voices penetrate my nightmares. I feel very agitated. Why won't they go away and let me sleep? The unmistakable sound of a bark filters into my subconscious; I try to shout, but panic halts the sound before I make it. Crawling over to the door, I ball my fist and bang. Weakness impedes the impact, but thankfully the dog senses my presence. A heavy, rhythmical banging follows;

the door opens, and there stands several police officers. As I slump slowly forwards, one of them makes a grab for me, narrowly breaking my fall.

'Who are you?' softly, kindly a policewoman asks.

I mumble, slurring, as I try to communicate my name. The policewoman understands me though. A policeman picks me up and the two of them carry me out to the waiting ambulance. After a small drink of water and a physical check, the crew drive me to hospital.

Lying in my bed, I am suddenly aware of voices I recognise, voices that are so dear to me - my darling Mum and Dad. They hug me gently while we all cry together. A few days later my dear friend Amber comes to see me. It had been agreed that she should be the one to explain what had happened to me.

'My husband Tony has searched everywhere for Matt. He hasn't been into work either. It's obvious he has packed up and left. He reported this to your parents who notified the police at once.'

'Has anyone checked out my cards, and bank?'

'Yes they were found to have large sums of money withdrawn.'

'The jewellery, has that been found?'

'It's all been sold to a not too reputable trader, I'm afraid.'

'The demolition of the building you were locked up in is due to take place in a couple of days. Thank goodness one of the watchmen's dogs picked up your scent through the gap at the bottom of the door. He alerted his owner who, when not able to find a key, phoned the police who came with a tracker dog. The rest you know. Thank heavens you are with us now!'

Tears run down Amber's cheeks as she hugs me.

'Will I ever be able to forgive myself for introducing you to that rat? When the police caught up with him they found it was the old, old story; drugs! He had got into debt and you, unfortunately, became a good target to get the money he needed. Tony said he is feeling dreadful because he must have let slip how wealthy your parents are.'

'Amber, you mustn't blame yourself, or Tony. And -- oh my goodness me! Because I was so excited about meeting that Matt, I forgot to bring your birthday present to your party, but Mum brought it into hospital for me to give you. Here is your birthday present with all my love.'

# The Wrong Road

Pulling up in the pub car park on her way home from work, Sarah walked into the bar and asked for a bottle of wine to take away, looking around as she waited for her order. She took a sharp intake of breath, when she spotted Callum in close conversation with two shady looking characters. Pulling herself together, she walked across to say hello to Callum. She suddenly became aware she had interrupted a heated conversation. Thumping the table, one of the men stood up glaring at her.

'Clear off! We're having a private conversation.'

Sarah stood there looking at Callum. Her eyes moved to look straight into the eyes of the man, then looked him up and down, waiting for Callum to defend her. But he sunk back into his seat with a worried look on his face. The other man glowered at Callum saying:

'You'd better put her right mate or you'll have trouble.' to which, sinking further into his seat. Callum said nothing.

Sarah couldn't believe what she was witnessing. Was Callum really such a weakling? Obviously he was. Giving Callum a look to kill, she turned on her heels, and walked out, shaking with anger.

Driving home, her mind was not entirely on the road as she travelled. She didn't notice Callum overtaking her until she had to slam her brakes on when he pulled up in front. Sitting there, while she recovered from her sudden braking, she was puzzled when Callum opened her passenger door and got in. She didn't like the strange look on what was normally his dear face. She liked even less what he said.

'Sarah, I'm sorry, but our relationship is finished. I can't continue seeing you.'

'What? What's this all about? I saw you in the pub just now with some blokes who didn't look at all nice. Are they the reason?'

'Partly, but just understand we're finished...end of story.'

'This can't be happening! Please come home with me so we can talk this over properly; and not sat in my car with a wind howling round us shaking the car and making it very cold.'

'Ok then. Lets go quickly and get it finished with.'

He shoved the door open, walked back to his car and they drove off to her parent's farm.

She went into her bedroom, where normally her eyes would have focused on the beautiful calming view across the hills. But today her sight was blurred with tears, and her heart was breaking. As she walked in, she wasn't sure if she would ever feel that calmness here again, after the bombshell Callum had just dropped.

Sarah's distraught mind couldn't help recalling the love and care her parents had heaped on her, and rightly or wrongly, she had expected this from Callum. Their support for her while she worked towards degrees in forestry, agriculture and horticulture was second to none. She now worked as an estate manager. It was in this roll that she had met Callum MacKenzie, the love of her life. The company he worked for sold and repaired farm machinery; needing a particular tool this was naturally the place to buy it. The pair of them locked eyes and that was that. They became an item. Both sets of parents were extremely happy to see their offspring so settled in a loving relationship.

Callum stood a few feet away with his head bowed, arms hanging at his side with fists clenched, knowing what he had done to her.

Sarah's face was white, her eyes glued to Callum, willing him to look at her so she could read his expression.

'I can't quite grasp this; exactly what is wrong? Have I done something to upset you, or have you met someone else? I need a reason,' she beseeched.

'No Sarah. It's not you, it's me. Sarah, I..I.. Oh God! How do I tell you? I have… well I'm in debt to the wrong people. I am in trouble, and they are getting nasty. I can't pay them back.'

His head shook from side to side, wishing he could be anywhere but here at this moment. To see Sarah so upset was tearing him apart even more than the verbal blow he had delivered.

'Callum how could you?' Sarah shouted, stamping her foot. 'We're engaged to be married and supposed to be saving to put a home together. This is so wrong. You really should have talked it over with me first.'

Walking over to the window, ignoring everything about the room, she turned and stomped back, closing in on him. Callum shuffled his feet, putting space between them before speaking.

'I needed some specialised tools. There is room for development in Drew's line of work, but the right tools are needed to do it. I would be the first in the area, which would make me top dog.'

'That's surely Mr. Drew's responsibility, not yours,' she stormed. 'Perhaps he doesn't want it that way.'

'Well I've done it now and I can't stop it; I don't want to be here anymore and that's all there is to it,' he said in a voice so icy cold it made her shiver involuntarily.

Sarah thumped one clenched fist into the other, wishing she were thumping Callum.

'You owe it to me to talk this over; there must be a solution. You don't have the God given right to blithely end our relationship, up sticks and walk. I'm worth more than that,' she sobbed.

Callum turned without a word, wrenched the door open and left, the door shaking the house behind him. Sarah threw herself on the bed sobbing into the pillow. When her sobbing abated and she had used half a box of tissues, she tried to rationalise, *he'll come back when he has calmed down. He's probably had a bad day at work.*

Several days passed without a word from Callum allowing nervousness to creep in. *I bet he's too embarrassed to contact me. Maybe I should give it a couple of days, and then ring him.* What Sarah didn't know was that because of his debt he had left home, rather than face the inevitable ructions there. Had she known about all this she could possibly have helped him. Sarah resolved, hard though it was, not to phone Callum before the couple of days had passed. Now her hands were trembling in anticipation as she punched the numbers into her phone. She sat there waiting anxiously for an answer, but to no avail. There was no reply, not even from his Mother. *Damn! I'll try his mobile* - this was unobtainable; she felt like throwing her phone on the floor. *Ah! Probably the transmitters are down due to the bad winds we had midweek.* Determined not to let herself get disheartened, she decided she'd got nothing on today so she would drive up to his house and find out what was happening.

Arriving at his parent's croft in Kilbride, Sarah rang the bell. There was no response; leaving her wondering if anyone was in. Pulling her coat tighter against the chilly wind, she was about to give up when his Mother answered the door, wiping her floury hands on her apron. Her hand flew to her mouth when she saw Sarah, and the tears started to roll down her unusually pale, drawn cheeks. She hastily wiped them away with her apron.

'Come in lass, come in.' Mrs. Mackenzie urged. 'My Callum has gone without a word and I d'nay know where!' Her tears ran again, profusely.

'Have you come with some news for me?' she asked hopefully. 'What with Hamish being away on the oil rig and men calling at the house asking for Callum and not giving a reason why, I'm beside myself,' Mrs. Mackenzie wailed, as she sank into a large armchair, with her head in her hands.

Sarah felt wretched and somewhat panicky at this outburst of grief. She walked across the room and sat on the arm of the chair, putting her arms round the distraught woman.

'Oh dear. No I haven't. I came here hoping to get some news from you. Did you know he had broken off our engagement? He has behaved in a very bad way, totally unlike the Callum I know and love,' Sarah gulped, hardly able to control her tears. 'I promise you I will do everything in my power to find out what is going on.'

Mrs. MacKenzie calmed down and insisted on making a cup of tea. She carried it in, together with a plate of freshly baked cakes. They sat eating and drinking in silence before Sarah said she really must leave before the dark clouds threatened to unload.

During her drive home, Sarah reflected on her relationship with Callum. He had always been such a warm, affectionate person; his appearance was that of a man's man, fit, and well built with strong, good-looking features. No wonder she had fallen for him; he was her dream man. They had spent many happy hours going for walks, meeting up with friends, joining in with village events - simply thoroughly enjoying each other's company. She recalled how passionate their relationship had always been; oh how she missed the physical contact.

Parking her car in Drew & Co. farm machinery company car park, where Callum had worked for six years, Sarah had an unpleasant tingle pass through her body. This was all too familiar, she realised. How many times had she done this, when going to either see or collect Callum? As she walked through the doors into the building, she subconsciously expected to hear the normal welcome from Callum. The memories were nearly more than she could tolerate. She was close to turning tail and running out when Mr. Drew, the proprietor, called out, warmly welcoming her; he had known her all her life.

'Well now young lady, what can I do for you? Come into the office where we can chat in peace.'

He put his arm across her shoulders and led her through the door. Feeling comforted by his attitude, Sarah sat down ready to open her heart about Callum.

'I've come on an unpleasant mission, Mr. Drew. Do you know the whereabouts of Callum?'

'Indeed I do not; and furthermore, I do not want to, after the way he has behaved. He was a good and trusted worker, for whom I had a lot of time.' declared Mr. Drew rising from his chair and stomping about the office in agitation. 'He walked out last Friday night and I've not seen hide nor hair of him since, and taking into account the mess he left me in, I don't want to. Added to all this I'm sick and tired of his creditors coming here every five minutes taking up my time, as if I haven't anything better to do; they needn't think I shall give them money. Let them track him down, my dear.'

He took out his handkerchief and wiped his nose in a contemplative way. He leant forward, taking her hand saying, 'now don't you go running about looking for him. He's not worth it, there are plenty more fish in the sea, and you could have any one of them; an attractive lass like you.'

Returning to the MacKenzie croft with this message for his poor mother, who became so stressed again, it made Sarah loathe leaving her on her own, but she needed to go home to sort out her own misery. She drove to Cleigh with a very heavy heart; sometimes hardly able to see where she was driving for the blur of her tears. On seeing her distress, her mother wrapped her arms around her, drew her into the living room, sat her down on the settee and waited for her tears to subside. 'I have a message from Iona.'

Iona was Sarah's friend and Mrs. Lamont wasn't sure it was the right thing to tell her of her friend's predicament, but came to the conclusion it could be just the answer for her daughter. Iona had moved to the Outer Hebrides to join her fiancé Blair, who had set up a tourist business running boat trips and attended to the administration and bookings. Sarah and Callum were due at Iona's wedding in three weeks time. It appeared she was in a bit of a state over the wedding. Her cousin, who was to be one of her bridesmaid's, had been taken ill; she wanted Sarah to ring her.

As soon as Sarah had calmed down and regained her composure, she rang Iona.

'Hello Iona, how are you? I'm so sorry to hear the news about your cousin. I hope she

recuperates soon. Has it messed you up too badly?'

'In a way yes. It will make the bridal entourage look unbalanced as I enter the church, and it's such a waste of a lovely dress.'

At this Sarah was sure of what was coming next.

'Would you consider taking her place? You are pretty well the same shape and dress size as Fiona, so please, please say yes?'

This was the last thing Sarah wanted to do in view of her present situation, but how could she say no to her dear friend?

'Iona, could I ring you back tomorrow when I have had time to get my head round this? You

see..., ' and she told Iona the demise of her relationship with Callum.

'Oh dear. I'm sorry. How horrid for you. You were such a lovely couple; yes take your time to think, then give me a ring.'

Once in bed, lying in the dark, with only the sound of the wind rattling the trees, Sarah spent a restless night mulling over Iona's situation. She hated the idea of going without Callum, yet knew she couldn't let her friend down. The next morning, when her father had gone off with the tractor and trailer to feed the cattle, she went downstairs still in a quandary, for a cup of tea and some toast, with the idea of talking over the matter with her mother.

'Mum,' Sarah said, as she put down her mug and wandered round the kitchen while she talked, 'I feel I need to do this for Iona. She has been a good friend over the years, plus I think I will apply for some holiday leave from work. I could turn the journey into a holiday by driving out to the Hebrides instead of using public transport.'

She looked at her mother for approbation, and seeing it, she continued; 'I shall do some sightseeing en route and book into a couple of guest houses, so I can relax. That will mean I can have some time with Iona before the wedding.'

Mrs. Lamont clasped her hands together, with a look of happiness on her face.

'Darling, that sounds like the perfect idea. It would give you a well-earned break. You've worked so hard lately and with this latest carry on, you really need a change of scenery and to have some girly time with Iona. Go for it, is what I say!'

While she was sorting out her clothes to pack, Sarah, still grossly unhappy about the turn her life had taken and desperately needing a change, suddenly thought, *I might even look for a new job in Stornaway. My CV reads well.* Then she worried about leaving her beloved parent's, yet knew they would be pleased for her if it lifted her heart.

She ran down the stairs to find her mum, who was just going out to collect eggs. Sarah grabbed another basket and followed her mother to help.

'Mum, what do you think if I left here and found a job in Stornaway?'

Mrs. Lamont gave a small gasp of surprise at her daughters proposed plan. Feeling she needed time to absorb this she turned to her daughter saying, 'You go out to the field where your father is feeding the cattle and ask him to come indoors while we discuss the situation. I'll go in and make us all a cup of coffee to go with the scones I've just baked.'

As she made the coffee and buttered the hot scones, Mrs. Lamont thought deeply about her daughter. She was their only child. They would miss her sorely, but she hoped they had brought her up to be able to stand on her own two feet.

Mr. Lamont kicked off his muddy boots in the porch way. He walked into the warm cosy farmhouse kitchen, inhaling the delicious cooking smells as they wafted up his nostril's.

'By gum, it's raw out there in the fields!' he said as he rubbed his hands and made his way to the brightly burning range. 'Now lass, what's all this "chat" business about. Have ye more problems?'

The three sat talking about Sarah's idea of relocating.

'Aye lass, if it's what ye want and think ye will be happy, then do it. If it d'nay work, well, ye know we're always here.'

'Thanks Dad. I was wondering what your opinion is on this... do you think that if a new job works out for me there, should I buy a house or rent a flat or house until I see if it works out?'

'I think ye shouldn't rush into purchasing until ye feel really settled. It could be a case of once the novelty has worn off, ye are not so keen and would rather be back here.'

By the time morning came, Sarah had made up her mind. Yes, she would go. She dialed Iona's number. When she answered Sarah said she would be happy to be her bridesmaid and went on to tell her of her planned journey and idea of job hunting. Then biting her bottom lip, feeling a little apprehensive:

'Would it be convenient to you if I were to arrive early and stay with you till the wedding? If not I could always book another guesthouse. It would give me a chance to look for a job.'

'Don't be silly! What are friends for? Of course you will be more than welcome to stay with us. We would love to have you here.'

Sarah was overjoyed at the welcome she heard in her friend's voice. She was starting to feel a little nervous as she and her parents were packing her Land Rover that had been thoroughly checked over. Her thoughts became clouded.

'I will be all right won't I? I'm quite used to driving on my own so why do I feel so apprehensive?'

'Of course you will darling,' said her Mum, and her Dad added,

'If ye no happy turn round and come back. Ye can always go by boat or plane. But ye'll be fine lass; ye'll do anything you put your mind to.'

They both hugged and kissed her and then she got into the vehicle and drove away.

With the aid of her map and armed with her "sat nav," Sarah drove towards Oban in order to pick up the coastal road. She wanted to be able to take in the views around Loch Linnhe. She noticed that the water of the loch looked quite smooth with just the odd ripple, reminiscent of satin fabric. After a while she decided to divert inland, so when she got to the crossroads she swung right, taking the road to Glencoe, where she looked forward to stopping for a rest and a cup of coffee. She knew the scenery was fabulous there.

Parking up, she reached into her bag for the flask and poured herself a cup of coffee. *Mmm,* she thought, *mum makes the best coffee.* Getting out of the car with her camera slung over her shoulder, Sarah stared in wonder at the beautiful scenery around her. She walked to the edge of the large parking area. She found herself looking at two vast mountains; one dropping to the right and one to the left, creating another valley where they met. Turning towards the right and looking down the glen, she could see that the road was nestled between the two mountain ranges that were coming down on either side of the glen. She went back to her car for a different camera lens and spent several minutes taking some memorable pictures. Several cars were parked in the parking area. It was obvious their occupants were just as awestruck. Sarah wandered over to a couple standing by their car, clearly enjoying the beauty surrounding them, and commented on the stupendous view.

'Stunning isn't it? You couldn't ask for much more natural beauty than this. I love it!' She said with a smile on her face.

'Yes,' they agreed. 'We're very lucky to live near here, and visit frequently. I'm Andrew Dudley and this is my wife Kirstie. Are you aware of the history of the "Glencoe Massacre" that took place in the year 1692?' asked Andrew.

'Yes I am,' she said, dragging her memory, 'but it was some years ago at school though. It's a problem remembering the details, other than I recall it was horrific. I have never actually been here before; thanks for reminding me. I will be aware of that as I travel. I know there is the military road they used for moving the troops around years ago. I'd like to spot that too. Isn't this an interesting area?'

'Oh look! Here's the piper who entertains the tourists,' said Kirstie, pointing to where a man in full Scottish dress was taking his bagpipes out of a car.

'Would you like my husband to take a photo of you with the piper, using your camera?'

'Yes please! You know, it doesn't matter how many times I hear bagpipes, I never tire of them; it's probably in my blood. The thought of this view and the music will sustain me for the rest of my journey. It has been a pleasure to meet you both. Oh, and by the way, I'm Sarah. Good Bye and thank you.'

Happy and relaxed as she drove towards the outskirts of Fort William, she lapped up more scenery as she went; perhaps too involved in the views, she swerved through lack of attention to her steering. Her heart leaped into her mouth because she came so close to the edge, she had to manoeuver the car back slowly, all the while hardly breathing, for fear of dropping into the river below. Then as she was almost there, some earth gave way. She braked and sat there, not daring to move, in case the car rocked and caused more earth movement. Her head dropped onto the steering wheel, and tears of fear started to drip onto the wheel. *What can I do?* She was too afraid to get out. As she sat trying to work out how to manage, a face appeared at the window. She gently wound it down, and the man said, ' don't worry lass; my friend and I are going to tow you back. Just sit tight and we'll sort it.'

After a breath holding half hour, the car was on safe ground. Sarah got out and thanked the men.

'I'm so grateful to you, I really don't know what I would have done without you,'

'Don't worry, my dear, we're only too glad to help a lady in distress. Think nothing of it. Get on your way and enjoy the rest of your trip.'

Getting back into the drivers seat Sarah had to force herself to stop shaking, but she couldn't help thinking what a handsome bloke one of the men was. *Shall I offer them a cup of coffee,* she wondered? Then thought, *no I'm not hear for involvement.*

The rugged mountains with the mist descending over their tops, the waterfalls with the shale at the bottom looking like a river, the sun slowly setting, giving the sky a beautiful red glow at the start of a gorgeous sunset, promised another lovely day tomorrow. 'How romantic.' Sarah said to herself; then mentally pulled herself up, as her thoughts drifted to her time with Callum. Those thoughts were not on the agenda. She refused to become upset again.

Arriving at her first overnight stop, “Highrock Guest House,” Sarah took her luggage out of the back of the car, climbed the steps to the door and rang the bell, which was opened by a plump, jolly lady.

‘Ah, you’ll be Sarah Lamont. Please come in. I’m Mrs. Duffy, your landlady. Just sign the guest book please. Then I’ll take you to your room.’

She made Sarah feel very at home with her cheerful chatter, while helping with her bags. Looking around her she was very pleased with what she saw.

‘What a lovely room, Mrs. Duffy, and just look at that view! Golly, I would like to stay here longer if I had the time.’

The room was cosily warm with pretty floral curtains and matching duvet, plus a lovely thick carpet that welcomed her feet; a wardrobe, a dressing table with a stool and a sumptuous looking arm chair, tea and coffee making facilities and even a small en-suite.

'Glad you like it, my dear. Now, dinner will be served in about three quarters of an hour, and that will give you time to freshen up. You will hear the gong.'

*'Ooh'* thought Sarah. *Mrs. Duffy's food smells gorgeous; I can't wait for dinner.*

Feeling refreshed after having a quick wash and brushing her hair, followed by a cup of coffee, she enjoyed the wonderful view from her window. Sarah emerged from her room and wandered down the stairs in search of the dinning room. When she entered, she saw there were six tables. Two were occupied by couples; one by four young men who gave the appearance of being walkers. All of whom acknowledged her. On the one next to hers, was a middle aged man, who just about managed a grunt in response to her cheerful, 'Good evening, my name is Sarah Lamont. May I know yours?'

'Mr. Boyd,' was grunted back to her with enmity. *Ah,* thought Sarah, *not the most sociable of people. Never mind; I shall enjoy my dinner and maybe be by the end of the meal the good food will have mellowed him a bit.* This was wishful thinking, Sarah was to find. Mr. Boyd was not a happy man, and was in no mood for company.

Arriving in the guest lounge Sarah took in the surroundings of warmth and comfort, which apparently were the keynote of the guesthouse. She went over to the table where there was a steaming pot of coffee and jug's, with the choice of cream or milk, plus a bowl of sugar crystals. Having just poured a coffee and about to sit down, she became aware of Mr. Boyd entering.

'Hello again. Would you like me to pour you a cup? Wasn't that a delicious meal? Mrs. Duffy did us proud.'

'Yes she did, and thank you, I will have a coffee. White, with no sugar.'

Sarah poured and took the cup over to Mr Boyd where he sat.

'This is my first visit here. Have you been before?'

'Yes once, and yes, Mrs. Duffy is a good landlady. Quite the little chatterbox aren't you?' He said morosely, shaking the newspaper he was holding. 'Now if you don't mind, I would like to read this paper, then get to my bed.'

'What a good idea. I've had a long journey as you probably have. Goodnight. See you at breakfast.'

Sarah was determined not to let his grumpiness ruffle her; she was in a happy mood. Revelling in the soft, warm water of the shower and mulling over her first day, Sarah was contented. *This trip is just what I needed,* she thought, allowing herself to feel a little smug. Having towelled dry and put on her PJ's, she loosely tied her mass of wavy brown hair back, then snuggled down into her comfortable bed. She closed her eyes and was just drifting off to sleep when she heard some strange, muffled, jangling noises coming from the next room that was occupied by Mr. Boyd.

Awakening refreshed after a good night's sleep, Sarah quickly showered and washed her hair, dressed in a pair of leggings, which showed off her lovely slender legs, pulled on a long, woollen tunic top, wound a bright scarf round her neck and slipped her feet into her boots. The smell of the breakfast cooking drifted up her nose as she descended the stairs, making her want to run to get there quicker. *Good grief! It smells as good as last nights dinner, I shan't want to leave here at this rate.*

'Good morning, Mr. Boyd. Did you sleep well?' she asked, as she entered the dining room.

'Yes thank you,' was his slightly more friendly tone of voice. 'Are you travelling far today? Where are you heading?'

'I have a long journey ahead of me. I have come from just outside Oban. I'm going to the Outer Hebrides for my friend's wedding, and I'm making the journey into a sightseeing holiday,' Sarah volunteered.

She was delighted the grumpy gentleman was ostensibly willing to talk. Maybe he could give her some information on the area she was going to travel to?

'Do you know the route I'm taking at all? Can you give me any tips?'

At this, Mr. Boyd shifted in his seat, feeling distinctly uneasy; it was not good that she was sight seeing!

'My advice is, whatever you do, don't go off the beaten track. You must be very careful. It is so easy to take the wrong roads. Follow your map religiously, don't deviate, and you will be alright,' he warned, in an almost sinister tone.

*Oops*, she thought *is he trying to put me off, or is he simply a bit of a Jonah?*

As they finished breakfast, they bid each other farewell, kitted themselves out for their long drives, thanked Mrs. Duffy, bid her goodbye and off they went on their different routes.

Sarah's planned journey was to take her alongside Loch Lochy and the famous Loch Ness. Would she see the monster? She could then pick up the smaller roads at Glen Urquhart, to take in the mountains and smaller lochs. Mrs. Duffy, bless her heart, had provided her with a generous picnic and refilled her flask, so when she got to some impressive, rugged scenery she stopped to have a snack. While she sat there enjoying her surroundings, she was thrilled when she caught sight of a pair of massive antlers emerging from behind a large rock. Sarah grabbed her camera, propped it on a piece of rock and waited. Her patience was rewarded. Eventually the truly majestic red deer, in all his glory, walked into full view. *Thank goodness for telephoto lenses,* she thought, as she snapped away, getting some enviable shots. Feeling very elated, she finally went back to her car. As she drove on, she entered the North West Highlands. *'Oh,'* she thought to herself, *'I'm so lucky to live in Scotland.'* Dusk was beginning to fall, so Sarah hastened her way to Glen Urquhart, where her next guesthouse was booked.

On arrival at Glen Urquhart, she finally found her lodgings. It was a lovely old house named "Rock Air". Grasping her bags, Sarah, rang the doorbell, and was welcomed into the house; it had the same warm and welcoming atmosphere as Mrs. Duffy's. Landlady Mrs. MacKay took her to her room. After a superb meal, followed by a glass of wine and a chat with other guests in the lounge, Sarah went to bed falling asleep as her head hit the pillow.

The next morning, during breakfast, she got into conversation with two men who introduced themselves as Ian and Ross. They were both young men, clearly dressed for walking. They were discussing the area.

'Are you here for rambling?' Ross asked her.

'No,' Sarah said. 'This is a sort of holiday sightseeing journey. I'm on my way to stay with a friend, so heading for the ferry at Ullapool. Yesterday I saw a beautiful red stag with superb antler's, and took some really good photos of him,' she told them excitedly.

'Why don't you take the more unusual roads? You would see some wonderful scenery and the photo opportunities would be something else,' said Ross.

Sarah mused on this and wondered whether she was brave enough. Ian, on seeing her slightly apprehensive look, taunted her saying, 'you don't strike me as being a scaredy cat. Go on. Have a go.'

She made up her mind to ignore her planned route and Mr. Boyd's sinister warnings, adopting a nonchalant air; no one was going to call her a scaredy cat; that was a challenge too far for her disposition.

Just as she was getting into her car, Sarah spotted a car arriving. It looked very much like that of Mr. Boyds. Oh well, probably not surprising; having discovered Mrs. Duffy and Mrs. MacKay were sisters. Perhaps a little strange he hadn't mentioned he was going this way, but then he may have taken a different route. Mr. Boyd was arriving as Sarah was leaving. He felt very anxious when he glimpsed Sarah's car, and was concerned she may have seen him; that would not do! He didn't want her to have any idea what his business was, and why he was here.

Dougal Boyd was a very dour man. His short slightly rotund build was not the best figure in the world for much walking, but he was committed to his assignment. He was worried when he couldn't see the car belonging to the people he was to meet; it caused him to pace about, and get more and more agitated. If they didn't hurry, they would miss their opportunity, and have to spend another day looking. He was about to go into the guesthouse for a cup of coffee, when at that moment the men arrived.

'You took your time,' Dougal said, belligerently.

The driver got out of his car, stretched his legs, reached for his jacket and putting it on and in an equally belligerent tone said,

'sorry, we got lost. It could happen to anyone, so don't go getting out of your pram, mate.'

'I'm Robert Downs and this 'ere is John Lang, so lets be going and talk on the way. Your car or mine?'

'We'll transfer the equipment from mine, and take yours,' said Dougal; quickly thinking, if they were unfortunate enough to bump into Sarah, she wouldn't recognise the car, and it was for business so why not use their petrol?

Sarah drove until she spotted a small road. It was pretty narrow, but the, "off the beaten track," roads were the general idea, so she could see some wildlife. Maybe she might even see a Golden Eagle. She was delighted that she had made the decision to make this a driving holiday. Being free to do as she pleased, it gave her a real feel good feeling, which she needed. The views were even better than she had hoped; so halcyon. Suddenly there it was! A Golden Eagle! What a magnificent bird! Sarah was utterly awestruck. When she regained her equilibrium, she hit the brakes, grabbed her camera bag and crept stealthily across the rough ground. Just as she got to a perfect position, the eagle took off. In the distance she saw it start to circle, so she hurried along, but it repeated it's annoying act of flying off.

'Damn you! You won't defeat me!'

She followed again. So determined was she to get the perfect shot, she completely lost track of both time and distance as she travelled over the rough terrain. Then her prayers were answered. The eagle suddenly appeared and with great aplomb, settled. She got a wonderful set of photos and hugged herself with total delight.

Coming out of her euphoria, Sarah realised the wind was increasing. Also darkness was descending and it was starting to rain. *Oh my goodness, I must get back to the car quickly. I've been too enthralled with what I'm doing and lost track of time,* she thought. As she stood up and looked around, she gave a gasp and clapped her hand to her mouth in shock. She hadn't got a clue as to which direction she should go! Panic started to set in. All she could do was to walk in the direction she thought she had come. Her walk became a stumble as she was getting wetter and colder, and the weather deteriorated. The wind became stronger and darkness was falling at an alarming rate. Sarah felt as though her clothes were being wrenched from her body by the wind. Just as exhaustion was about to beat her, she saw what she was convinced was ostensibly a building. This gave her a much needed boost of strength to carry on. When she reached the ramshackle building, she dragged herself in and dropped onto the floor, completely drained, and fell asleep.

Arousing from her sleep, Sarah realised she was open to the elements, so she picked up her bag and walked further into the building. It turned out to be a small derelict castle. The way she was feeling at the moment, she didn't care, so long as she had shelter. Her clothes were soaking wet and she was very hungry. After rummaging in her camera bag, she found a bar of chocolate, together with a few sweets. Having devoured these, she felt very thirsty, but of course her flask, along with everything else, was in the car. On scouting about, Sarah discovered that other people, who had used the building before, hadn't taken their rubbish home. Amongst it was an empty fruit tin.

'Great!' she exclaimed loudly. 'I'll catch some rain water in this.'

Having quenched her thirst, tiredness was overtaking her again, so she curled up as comfortably as possible, although her clothes were still quite damp, and once more fell asleep.

Later, Sarah woke with a start. It was still pitch black, but she could hear noises. On listening intently, she thought it must be owls or even bats, so she relaxed and dropped back off to sleep.

Dougal and his clients, Robert and John, arrived at the derelict castle. This was easy for Dougal. He knew a direct route there and the darkness didn't worry him. In fact it was perfect for his business. The Golden Eagle and Eagle Owl eggs! The one thing that would have been a problem had completely cleared up - the atrocious weather.

Robert and John were two Spivey type men, who had little regard for anything except lining their own pockets. They were in good company with Dougal in that respect. He had brought them to a perfect area for their gains; this was clearly why he had tried to persuade Sarah from using roads off the beaten track. Dougal had taken the two men to a perfect area for their booty; they were well equipped for the climbing.

As they entered the castle, the three men had such a shock when they came across Sarah, lying there fast asleep. Dougal was angry to discover her, but Robert, a lascivious character, was almost salivating at the sight of such a beautiful female, lying there so defenseless in her sleep. The men moved to a different place, in order to not disturb Sarah. They discussed their plan of action. Dougal and John were eager to get going and get away. All Robert wanted to do was to satisfy the lust Sarah had aroused in him.

'You go and sort out all the equipment, because that's quite a long job, while I stay here and make sure this young lady doesn't wake up and disrupt our aims,' he said in an innocent tone.

'Okay, so long as you realise how long it will take with only two of us, but maybe you're right. It would be safer for someone to watch over her,' agreed John.

*Good* thought Robert *the longer the better*. With that, the two departed and Robert raised a sigh of relief and made for Sarah. Before she was able to waken and restore her senses, he had managed to gag her. She came to in a haze and struggled to protect herself. As he ripped open her already tatty clothing, exposing her lovely body, he grew more aroused as he fondled her. She fought and kicked trying to scream, but the gag made that impossible. He was a strong man and the sight of her body plus her attempt to fight him off made him even more lustful. As Sarah's strength was ebbing, Robert raped her in a rough, greedy way, having thought for only his delights.

After he had satisfied himself, tidied his cloths and regained his self control; he went to find the other two as if nothing untoward had occurred, leaving her absolutely ravaged. She fell into a deep faint from shock and pain.

The Eagle Owl, an enormous bird and one to have respect for; it's eggs, because the adults nest in a hollow in the ground, were not difficult find or to steal. When the trio got there, the male was off hunting prey, so it wasn't very hard to frighten the female off the creamy white eggs. She then feigned injury to try and attract the predator, but John knew this trick. Having achieved their aim, they made for the Golden Eagles' nest, eager to reach there before dusk. The men were hoping the distinctive beige, white and brown dappled eggs hadn't hatched. If they had, they could still trade the chicks, but it was not as profitable a trade as the eggs. When they got to where the huge nest was up high on the rocks, luck was on their side. The parents had left the nest, the male to hunt, but the female was sitting on a rock further away watching. John volunteered to climb up. They had good equipment, so he climbed up using his ropes without too much of a problem. He was relieved to see they had not hatched, but was querulous because Dougal and Robert were not doing a good job of keeping a watch out for the parents. Their beaks and claws looked frightening. He was afraid of the damage they could do to him. Eventually he managed to get the eggs, but in his rush to get away he nearly dropped one, but succeeded getting all of them into the pouch, which he lowered down to Robert.

The three evil men made their way back to the castle, pleased with their booty, metaphorically rubbing their hands at the money they would make. Dougal had another area he planned to take them, for their ill-gotten gains.

When reaching the castle, Robert offered to stow away their pickings. He was worried about the reaction of the others, if they were to gather what he had done. He almost had a conscience about it, realising how stupid he had been. Perhaps he should have gone into check on her and let them put the eggs away, but it was too late now. The pair were horrified to see Sarah, gagged and virtually naked in her ripped clothes, huddled up in a corner. Her eyes were wide with fear, trying to screw up her body hoping to be less obvious. She was terrified at their appearance; so afraid of what would happen to her now. Would they also rape her? She was terrified when Dougal bent down to gently ungag her. Placing his coat over her he demanded.

'Who did this to you? We haven't seen anyone else about.'

Sarah just remained huddled up pressing into the corner, still afraid of what might become of her. She felt filthy and so repulsed by what had happened to her. She burst into tears again and when Dougal tried to put his arm round her to comfort her, she pushed him away in horror. Dougal asked again who had inflicted this crime on her?

'It - it was your friend! He - he raped me! Please help me!I don't know where my car is and I want to go home; please help,' she gasped out between sobs, repeating, 'I don't know where my car is, I'm so cold and I feel ill.'

Dougal had thought of Sarah as a nuisance before, but would never have wished this on her. She was a harmless person.

John, furious at what had happened, went out to find Robert. When he did, he gave him such a pasting; the wretch didn't know what day of the week it was. John felt total disgust for his colleague. As far as he was concerned, this was definitely the end of any association with him. He would love to leave the wretch here to find his own way back, but it would make him as bad as Robert, so he tied his hands behind his back and shoved him into the back of the car. Dougal, aided by John, got Sarah to her feet and took her to the car, where they helped her into the front, wrapping a rug round her.

'My camera,' she shouted, 'please get it.'

John did this, placing it on her lap. Dougal, knowing which was the right track, drove down until they spotted Sarah's car. She was too distraught to drive, so having made sure Robert was too secure to cause any problem, John drove it, following Dougal, who took Sarah to the nearest doctor. He went into the surgery first to explain the situation. A nurse went out to the car and helped Sarah into the doctors surgery. The doctor was very gentle and kind to her, talking all the while he was examining her and taking various DNA samples and other necessary swabs, which were dispatched straight to the laboratory. The nurse showed Sarah where the shower was. She scrubbed and scrubbed, but still felt dirty and was sobbing her heart out. Her lovely holiday was ruined. What was she going to do? All she really wanted was to get home to her parents. The doctor phoned the police, who came straight away and took statements from everyone. Again they were understanding and kindly to Sarah. They arrested Robert and insisted that Sarah was to go to hospital for a complete check, before she went home. The nurse had been to Sarah's case to get fresh clothes for her to travel in. The police needed her dirty ones for forensics. She then organised a hospital car to collect her. It was such a sad end to her holiday and a bitter disappointment that she wouldn't get to her friends wedding in Stornaway.

Sarah's mum arrived to collect her from the hospital; she was in tears as she hugged her daughter. Leaning heavily on her mother, they walked out to the car. Sarah opened the car door, and a voice she recognised so well at once greeted her.

'Hello darling,' it was Callum...

Once back home the couple went up to Sarah's room. She sat on the bed, twisting and wringing her hands, doing all she could to not break down again. They spent an hour sitting there, with Callum's arms around her, doing his best to comfort her. He assuring her that her terrible experience didn't make any difference to his feelings for her, other than his deep sorrow for what she had suffered, and if he got his hands on the bloke he felt he would kill him. They then discussed their feelings for each other. Were they still the same after the recent happenings? The culmination was, their love for each other was as strong as it had always been, but they realized the biggest problem was Callum's debt and his lack of a job. Luckily, although Sarah had seriously thought about going to work in

Stornaway, she hadn't actually given her notice in, thus still had employment.

Callum had had a guilty conscience after he had left his life behind. He deeply regretted the hurt and upset he had caused both Sarah and his family. Finally he plucked up the courage to contact the police; they had caught and taken the creditors to court.

Eventually the couple went down to join Sarah's parents, who both had worried looks on their faces.

'Is there a problem for you? Have you not reached an agreement?' Mrs. Lamont anxiously asked when seeing their faces.

'It's my situation that is the problem,' said Callum, feeling embarrassed.

'Oh if that's all, then there aren't any worries,' boomed Mr. Lamont, who then proceeded to tell them that he and Callum's dad had paid off his debt, which they would expect Callum to repay to them, but obviously minus the interest. Also that he had been to see Mr. Drew, who was prepared to give him another chance, due to him being brilliant at his job.

The couple exchanged looks of disbelief. Coupled with the utmost gratitude, they hugged each other in total relief. Sarah went to her dad and gave him a great big hug, while Callum shook his and his own dad's hands, gently banging them on their backs. Sarah and Callum both had tears in their eyes,

'Ah, that's not all my dears. There's one more thing,' said Mrs. Lamont. 'You are both booked on the seaplane for Stornaway next week, in time for Iona's wedding!'

Hilary Forde

# Hush

# Hilary Forde

Four close friends were sitting by the welcoming inglenook fireplace in their local pub. They felt cosy and happy as they sat sipping their drinks, and watching the flames flickering warmly from the burning logs. A feeling of content flowed over each at the thought of a holiday. Weariness was taking over. They were all experiencing a busy time lately. Yve and Dave Brandon with their successful business producing medical instruments. Amy and Neil West, as much sought-after accountants. Sitting there they all agreed on the need for a lazy, slow-paced holiday in the countryside, where everyone could relax and unwind in the fresh air. Yve offered to look up some self-catering holidays; ideally a comfortable farmhouse in Mid Wales.

Finding a website was no trouble. A perfect farmhouse came on the screen in Radnorshire; it was an isolated hill farm, surrounded by enviable scenery.

'Dave,' she called. 'Have a look at this. It looks perfect.'

'My goodness, yes it does. Why don't you send for the brochure straight away? I'm sure the other two will love it,' Dave enthused after he had read the details.

The brochure arrived within three days. Armed with the literature, Yve met Amy for lunch at a small but popular restaurant in town. The two men had agreed that if the farmhouse appealed to the girls, then it was good enough for them and they gave them a free hand to book it. Yve and Amy sat pouring over the brochure with odd gasps of delight.

'It looks like the only neighbours we shall have are sheep,' said Yve with a giggle while waiting for their food. The girls were thrilled at the prospect.

'This couldn't be more perfect; the house looks lovely doesn't it? It's so snug nestled into the hill rock, and just look at those views,' Amy said. 'It appears to be nicely secluded.'

'Ideal too, because we wouldn't be too far from the areas and places we would like to visit, such as The Elan Valley, Llandrindod Wells spa town and rock park as well as Corris Centre for The Alternative Technology. That's if we're not too lazy to travel around. I love it! I have a feeling we will be very happy there.'

'Well the boys have given us free gratis, so lets go ahead and book before someone else books the two weeks we want in early September.'

Just then their meals arrived.

'Ooh this looks lovely,' said Amy, as she almost drooled over her plate of a full rack of ribs and chips.

'It certainly does. Perhaps this is a good omen for our holiday,' Yve replied as she cut into the ribs.

When Yve got back to her office, and before she did anything else, she got the brochure out of her bag, sat down, and dialled the house owners. She made the booking, and paid the deposit. She had such a good feeling about this holiday, it put her on a high for the afternoon. Dave was thrilled it was all sorted and phoned Neil to let him know. Neil was equally happy.

As time drew nearer to departure, Yve and Dave had invited their friends to dinner one evening. The idea was to do a final check. Having finished dinner, Yve took their glasses and the bottle of wine into the lounge where she and Amy could start drawing up a list of things required for self-catering. They decided against taking food as space was at a premium, but a few non-perishable items would be good to take. The next thing on the agenda was clothes shopping.

'No, definitely no,' Dave and Neil said in unison at the girls suggestion.

'This is a holiday to relax, and not worry about our appearance. One of the reasons we decided on this holiday was to chill out. And that includes not having to dress up. We wear suits all week, and we will be in the country out in the sticks where we will be free to do as we please,' Neil said.

'But we will be doing some touristy things,' Yve argued. 'We need to look reasonable for that, and if we eat out at any point which we will do occasionally because we girls don't intend to be slaves to the oven while on holiday,' continued Yve.

'We do that all the other weeks of the year,' Amy chipped in with feeling.

Dave and Neil looked at each other with raised eyebrows.

'We can do our share,' Dave said, beginning to think the holiday may not be as relaxed as he had hoped. The boys were still non-committal; they were clearly going to need more persuasion.

'Yve, how about making a nice cup of coffee, while Neil and I work out what equipment we may need,' said her husband, hoping to defuse the situation.

'Make it yourself,' Yve almost snarled. 'I'm not your slave.'

'Do you get the message, Neil?' said Dave with a laugh in his voice.

As he spoke he raised questioning eyebrows at Neil for approbation. Receiving a slight nod from his pal, Dave went to Yve and put his arm around her, nuzzling into her neck.

'Okay, you win darling; new clothes it is, but not bank-busting shopping,' he conceded.

As usual the girls won the day, and off they went to the large department store. After making a variety of purchases, they decided on a coffee.

'I feel like being really naughty Amy, do you? Shall we nip into that new boutique? Just to have a look.'

'Why not! Come on, have you finished your coffee?'

Yve swigged down the last mouthful and grabbed her bags; they both almost waltzed out of the restaurant in excitement. They weren't going to buy anything, of course.

Neither knew who was worse. They both came out of the boutique feeling guilty, with bags of lovely bright summery maxi dresses, shorts and T-shirts. In order to salve their conscience, they popped back into the men's department of the large store to purchase shorts and T-shirts for their husbands.

'This is almost as much fun as the holiday will be,' Yve said with a wicked grin. Amy gave her a friendly push as she nodded and laughed in agreement.

While their wives were shopping, Dave and Neil checked the car. That finished, Dave went indoors and grabbed a couple of beers from the fridge for them to enjoy on the patio while they made some travel plans. The consensus of opinion had been to use Dave's car, as it was a large four-wheel drive. Neil suggested they get out the maps to plot the journey.

'I think we should take the scenic route. It will make it part of the holiday and probably a more relaxing drive.'

Dave agreed.

That night when they eventually got to bed after packing their suitcases, Yve snuggled up to Dave.

'I think this could be the best holiday we have ever had. So peaceful and relaxing, don't you think so darling?' she said, gently stroking his face.

'Mmmm,' was Dave's reply as he dropped off to sleep.

Yve and Dave loaded their luggage and made their way to their friend's home. The wives elected to travel in the back, leaving the men to do all the boy's stuff. The music was resonating from the CD player, and they were all singing along to it loudly, full of the joys of the anticipated holiday. The journey progressed and as they left the English roads for the Welsh, their spirits soared even higher when looking around at the mountainous scenery.

'I'm so glad we chose this part of the country and well done to you boys for choosing the scenic route. It has been a great start to the holiday,' Amy said in a lazy, contented tone.

'I'll second that,' came Yve's rejoiner.

'By golly, we've done something right!' Neil mocked. 'Ouch!' he exclaimed, rubbing his shoulder as he received a retaliating thump from his wife.

They were now approaching Rhayader. Yve and Amy kept squealing in alarm when the odd sheep nonchalantly wandered across the road, completely oblivious of vehicles.

'The grass is always greener,' Dave said.

Reaching their destination they were overjoyed by the lovely old stone house. While the boys unpacked the car, Yve and Amy did a tour of the house. They were delighted with what they saw. The girls plumped for the two front bedrooms; the beds in both rooms were positioned to give the users terrific views out of the windows. Amy gave a little squeal when she went into the large bathroom, which was in between the two bedrooms.

'You can lie in the bath and look at the view while you wallow. How spoilt can you be?'

There was ample accommodation, which included a farmhouse kitchen with an AGA. And to the boys delight, a wood-burning stove in the large lounge. There was even a boot room. They quickly settled in and unpacked their luggage before they cooked the dinner.

'Isn't it nice to be able to cook and eat leisurely instead of racing around after a days work,' said Amy as they all sat finishing their off their wine.

They all shared the clearing up, loaded the dish washer, then the four of them collected their bits and pieces to chill out on the patio with a bottle of wine.

'Listen to the silence,' Yve said.

All they could hear were the bats flying about. They sat contentedly sipping their drinks, contemplating their plan of action.

The next two days were spent visiting various tourist areas, including the Elan Vally. This was where in the late seventeenth, early eighteenth century, massive reservoirs were built to supply water to Birmingham. The many large dams were a marvellous sight, attracting tourists “en-masse.” A small village had been evacuated because it had to be flooded to allow the course of the necessary reservoirs. When the water level was low, it was possible to see odd bits of the old village.

‘My mind runs riot,’ said Yve. ‘I can’t help feeling for those people even though they were re-housed.’

‘I know what you mean,’ agreed Amy, ‘it makes me feel creepy. Let’s find the boys and go home.’

They had been long and tiring days so they decided today they would take it easy. After a lazy breakfast the two wives made a flask of coffee, collected rugs and cameras and walked up the tracks to a high grassy area, where they’d decided to spend the morning taking in the views of the surrounding mountains. It was a great vantage point for photographs. Neil and Dave had gone to check their maps for future trips and said they would join the girls when they had finished.

'Phew!' exclaimed Amy as they reached the top, 'that's quite a trek isn't it, but well worth it 'cause you can see for miles between those mountains.'

She stood looking around, thrilled with what she could see. The pair spread the rugs and flopped down, exhausted after their trail up the long hill. All they could think of, for a while, was to lie and absorb the sun, air, bird songs and glorious blue sky.

Once they had rested and recovered from their walk, they sat up to have a cup of coffee. Looking at her watch, Yve was surprised by how much time had gone past since they had laid down.

'Our men folk are taking their time,' she observed.

'Aren't they! I bet they've been exploring and lost track of time. Never mind, the coffee is still hot. They'll come when they're ready. I just want to lie here and take everything in, it's so lovely.'

Finishing off their coffee, they lay back down and were dozing when they heard what, at first, sounded like a low flying aeroplane. Yve was puzzled knowing this wasn't a flight path. As the sound got louder, the next thing they saw was a low flying helicopter appearing over the mountains.

'It must be a private flight,' Yve said lying back down to resume her nap.

'Oh my god!' Shouted Amy, pure panic in her voice, to which Yve leaped up, looking to where Amy pointed.

'It's in trouble! Yve look! The tail rotor has stopped. It's in serious trouble.'

The girls clutched each other, screaming as they watched, unable to believe what they were seeing; the machine was spinning and dropping out of the sky. It came down on the farmhouse.

'The boys!' Yve screamed, 'the boys...where are they? Please don't let them have been in the house!'

Amy, struggling to regain her senses, grabbed Yves hand as they raced down the tracks towards the house. It was obvious they couldn't get near. The helicopter was exploding like an enormous firework, with flames shooting everywhere, and detritus from the building was tumbling about. There was an enormous groan and noise as they saw the remainder of the roof fall in. The wives stood there, totally dumfounded by what they were witnessing. Then sense came to them.

'Phone the emergency services!' shouted Amy.

Yve shouted back, 'We can't. The mobiles are either in the house or the car, and that's on fire too.'

'Can you remember how far the nearest house is?' yelled Amy.

'No, I'm going to see if there is any way I can get into the house. I'm sure the boys are in there, or they would have seen it and come back by now if they were anywhere else. Her face was distorted by dread and panic. Her husband must be alright. She would find him.

'You can't, Amy. It's far too dangerous,' Yve shouted as she tussled with Amy who was a lot stronger than she looked.

Frantic to stop her friend going into the inferno she gained strength she didn't know she had.

'Let's shout and see if we can get a response.'

They shouted until they were hoarse, but got no response; finally collapsing onto the ground. In floods of tears, not knowing what to do, they heard the fire, ambulance and police claxons as the vehicles roared down the track. Amy and Yve ran to the firemen, their arms flailing, screaming at them to find their husbands.

While the firemen fought to extinguish the ferocious flames intensified by the helicopter's fuel, two women constables tried to console the girls, but the only thing they could think of was finding their husbands. They struggled to get free of the constables' restraints, intent on the idea of getting into the building. Yve finally managed to slip free and raced towards the remains. A fireman with breathing apparatus was able to block her, and although she fought with all her strength, she couldn't get past him, and finally crumpled in surrender. The firemen carried her out to Amy where the pair just clung to each other. Both were now beyond tears.

The silence was dreadful until a shout went up.

'Make way! We've found them!' The girls ran forward with a mixture of eagerness and fear, their faces contorted with anxiety while the doctors and paramedics got on with their jobs.

One of the doctors went to Yve and put his arm around her shoulders.

'I'm afraid your husband didn't survive his multiple injuries,' he told her.

Yve let out a heartbroken howl and fell to the ground at the news, sobbing her heart out. She struggled up and forced her way over to her husband's lifeless body and lay across him, talking to him and caressing him, until a nurse carefully pulled her away. Neil, although badly burned and injured was still just alive. Amy stood by him, numb and in total shock. She ached with the need to hold him, but wasn't able to due to the burns and broken bones he had suffered when some beams had fallen on them. She felt the need to comfort her friend but couldn't tear herself from her husband.

The police phoned for counsellors to come and help the girls, who had lost everything. One of the counsellors, Mary, set about sorting out a hotel room, a change of clothes and toiletries but the girls were too distraught to bother about any of that. Amy just wanted to be with her husband. She was allowed to go to the hospital with him in the ambulance and the paramedic worked non-stop protecting his burns and injuries. She also had to tend to Amy, who was showing signs of shock. Neil was sedated, but in so much pain he was groaning all the time. Yve was so beside herself, she kept asking for her mother June, who arrived within a few hours. She had seen the accident on the news, so had packed a case and left at once. A counsellor had stayed in the hotel room with Yve and the doctor had sedated her, but she was still traumatised. When her mother arrived, Yve became a little less distressed, taking great comfort from her mother.

'I'll give your daughter another sedative to calm her down and help her to sleep,' the doctor told June as he filled a syringe. June lay cuddling Yve all night. In the morning, Yve knew she had to go and see Amy, who was staying at the hospital until Neil was off the danger list. They met in an anti-room, as only Amy was allowed into her husband's room at the moment. Both girls hugged each other sobbing; neither could speak for a long while. A message had been sent to Amy's parents who were due in two days; they were travelling back from a trip to America. Until then, both Yve and June felt that they must be there for Amy. It was also good for Yve to have to think of something other than her own bereavement, which would have dragged her down.

A few days later Yve and her mother went to the hospital to see Amy and Neil, who was improving enough to have visitors for a short time. Yve couldn't believe the state of her friend's husband who was scarcely visible through all the bandaging. She had enormous difficulty in staying put. She could hardly bear the sight of her friend in that state. Neil's injuries were severe. His burns would need grafts and his left leg had had to be amputated above the knee as it was so badly smashed; his broken right arm wasn't a complicated break and would mend, as would his broken ribs. He also had a nasty gash on his head which was causing some concern. Amy never left his side while he was in hospital. He intermittently groaned and writhed in pain and the nurse would administer strong painkillers. When these took effect he became almost his old self, chatty and laughing. During the bad times, she sat there praying, wishing she could take the pain for him. The worst part of it all was that Neil couldn't and wouldn't accept his leg had been amputated. As with many physically active men, this was an enormous blow and usually often the patient couldn't come to terms with it for a long time.

When Neil was having treatment that would take a few hours, Amy would hurry out of the ward and go to see Yve. Her friend was beginning to cope with her situation by plunging herself into work almost twenty-four/seven. This made her look gaunt and grey; a shadow of her former self. Her mother had to temporarily return home. She had to sort out their house, then she and Yves dad were coming back to help with the funeral. Both parent's were beginning to worry about her even more; they felt there was something else wrong with their daughter.

On the day of Dave's funeral Yve went through the motions in a complete daze. Her parents had organised all of the arrangements, but had no idea there would be so many people attending. Dave and Yve, a popular couple, had made a lot of friends through Dave's business. Amy, determined to put her troubles to one side for that day, was at her friends' side along with Yve's parents. Somehow, Yve got through the day, but all in a bit of a haze. Everybody was so kind and even though she managed to put on a brave face, she just wanted to be left alone to mourn in her own way.

Two days later Yve knew she had to pull herself together. Her beloved husband had worked so hard to build up the business with the idea that once it was secure they could start a family.

'Huh!' she said aloud. 'Fat chance of that now.'

For all that had happened, she couldn't possibly let Dave's hard work go under. She had worked alongside him, so knew the trade completely; she was determined to keep it going.

A week later, relieved that Neil was showing signs of progress and had at last acknowledged the amputation, although not accepting he would be restricted for a while, he had realised how devoted Amy had been. He could see she was deteriorating herself and he insisted she took some time out.

'I will be alright darling, really. You go and do something for yourself for a change.'

'If you are sure dear, I would like to go and get my hair cut and maybe I could call on Yve. I know she is digging into the business, but I worry in case she overdoes it. She has had a terrible shock and like us, has to make a new life for herself.'

'That would be lovely darling. When you see her please give her my love and tell her I'm thinking of her.'

Amy felt like a different person once her hair had been cut and blow dried. She then went to a gift shop and bought a delicate china ornament for her friend; then to an off-licence to purchase what she knew was Yve's favourite wine.

Arriving at Yves house, she knocked on the door. When Yve opened it, Amy was quite shocked to see how her friend appeared to have shrivelled up. They hugged, and all Amy could feel was a mass of bones. They went into the kitchen to put the wine in the fridge and Amy gave her the ornament, but she just didn't know what to say to her friend as she was simply a shadow of the person she knew. Trying to pull herself together, Amy briefly gave an account of Neil's condition and his rehabilitation, but at the back of her mind was that she had to get Yve to see what she was doing to herself. She could completely understand what was happening, but she also knew that it had got to stop, or Yve would be joining her husband. Broaching the subject she could see Yve stiffen up in defence, but she carried on.

'Yve you have simply got to see what you are doing to yourself. Please remember you have got friends who will do anything to help, so please let us. If you don't, you are on a downward slope and that has only one ending. I hate to say it, but would Dave have wanted this? He was so proud of his business and thrilled that you enjoyed working with him.'

Yve sat quietly mulling over what Amy had said. She knew she was only confirming what her own mother had said and what she really knew herself. She was giving way to her own grief. Neglecting the upset she was causing those around her. She knew she needed help with the business, but until now – this minute, she hadn't been able to work out what to do about it. Yve suddenly had a brilliant idea. She gasped. Leant forward and grabbed her friend's arm with a smile on her face; which was a rare thing these days.

'Amy, would you consider coming into the business and working with me? That way you'd be able to earn and look after Neil as well.'

Amy's eyes opened wide with surprise, and with her hand at her chin she pondered the thought for a few minutes, working out the possibilities. She could see that it could well work.

'Yve what a wonderful idea. That would be marvellous. It would give Neil somewhere different to be other than just sitting in the house.'

'I also wondered whether Neil would be able to take on the accounts while he recuperates, and all being well, stay on with the company as our accountant. That would be an enormous help.'

'What a great idea! It would keep Neil's mind busy, which could prevent him getting too depressed about his injuries.'

Amy looked at Yves face; it had come alive for the first time since the terrible events of that summer.

There was a hush in the room as they instinctively, but momentarily recalled the accident. Then the silence was broken as they chinked their glasses to a new beginning.

It was more of a new beginning than they had anticipated. Yve was not feeling too well and Amy feeling concerned, wanted to march her off to the doctors, but Yve stoutly refused to go. Yve insisted that her malady was down to shock still coming out and probably she was overdoing things at work, although Amy and Neil had taken a lot off of her shoulders. She missed Dave desperately, and at times wondering whether she could go on without him. That morning on getting out of bed she felt so sick and light headed, she had to lie down again. She rang Amy to say she would be late in. After she had been in bed all day feeling sick. Sense told her she should go to the doctor as she didn't seem to feel any better. Maybe he could give her something to stop the queasiness so she could get on with life. When he had examined her; the doctor sat back down. He indicated for her to do so.

'Hmm, you obviously haven't realised you are pregnant. Is that going to give you a problem?'

'Pardon?' she questioned. 'Pregnant? I can't be! Dave has been dead for three months,'

With that she clapped her hand over her mouth. Her face colouring to a gentle red.

'Oh my goodness – yes it is possible – what am I three months or more?'

'You are indeed my dear. How do you feel about it?'

'Happy, but at the same time a bit sad, it will be a piece of Dave, but he will never see his own child. He would have loved it.'

'Well we must take great care of you and the baby. Now go home. Tell your Mother, and your friend, but most importantly look after yourself.'

Yve rang her Mother who was beside herself with delight.

'A grandchild! That's wonderful darling! Your father and I will come to see you, and help you sort things out.'

'That would be lovely Mum. Thank you.'

Putting the phone down she went and made herself a cup of tea, and took it with her to ring Amy.

'Amy, have you got time to pop round? I have something to tell you.'

'Of course dear. There's nothing wrong is there?'

'Not wrong. I just need to talk to you.'

'I'll be there within half an hour. I'll just sort out his nibs and then come.'

True as her word Amy was tapping at the door twenty minutes later.

'Right my lady. What do you need to say to me?'

'Amy, I haven't felt too bright for a couple of days; you know a bit nauseous, so I went to the doctors, and – you'll never guess. I'm pregnant!'

Amy sat down suddenly. Her mouth dropping open.

'How? When? I don't understand.'

'Now Amy don't tell me you don't know how babies are made, but seriously I am pregnant. Nearly four months pregnant, and I don't know whether to laugh or cry! A baby Amy. A little piece of Dave!'

The girls hugged each other in delight, and again hush reigned

'Do you think we can cope Amy?' she asked cautiously, not entirely sure of her friends reaction.

'Of course we will. You have no worries there. That baby will be so loved by all of us.'

**Hilary Forde**

# My Son the Soldier

He stealthily crept down the stairs while pulling on his jacket, carefully missing the creaky one. He stopped by the door and bent down to pick up his shoes, to put on when he reached the path. John had a problem to shut the door fearing his mother would hear it. He'd always thought she had robotic ears. John's dread was that his mother would suspect what his mission was. If she did he was sure she would scupper it. He was determined to join the army. Life was not easy if, like him, you'd left school with no qualifications, and no ambition to go to university; his mother's deepest wish.

*What a hard job it is being a mother. I have done all I can, helping, and encouraging John to work hard at school. He thinks I don't know his plan to join the army, but like all mothers I am one step ahead of him. I know what makes him tick. When his father gets home on leave he will be thrilled. I will have no back-up.*

*For me it is bad enough having a husband who has done all the dangerous stuff, and survived. You would think I was used to it, but no; I don't want my son there.*

Arriving at the recruitment centre he filled in numerous forms. Next he took tests, and had talks with several service recruitment staff. Then he went into a darkened room to watch a DVD about training, and what it would be like to be in the field. The idea of this was to depict the rough, and the smooth, to prevent glamorisation of the role of a service person.

'This is not new to me Sir. I have heard it from my father Sir.'

'Then I take it your father has told you the bad that happens, because bad it can be.'

'He certainly has Sir, but he still loves it Sir. To him it is all part of the job he loves Sir.'

'It sounds as though you haven't been sheltered lad. And you're still keen?'

'I really am Sir. I want this more than anything Sir.'

What it did do was enforce his love of the life. He joined the army there and then. Going home and telling his mum was the hardest part. He found it impossible to keep the joy out of his voice.

'Mum, I've done it. I've join the army. Please be happy for me. It's all I have ever wanted to do.'

'Oh John, I'm pleased you are so happy, but please understand it makes me very nervous with all the theatres of war going on. But if you're happy, then I would be a poor mother if I wasn't happy too. My main thought is that you take care.'

John hugged his mum, and assured her he would be very careful, and thanked her for her support.

It seemed no time before he was at Salisbury Plain for his training. He loved every minute of it. He was reliving everything his dad had told him. His father would be so proud of him. Once his training was finished John went home for some leave. His mum Ann was happy to see him, thinking how well he looked. It was quite clear that the life suited him.

Upon his return to his barracks he had one of the greatest thrills of his life. He was being deployed to Afghanistan with his unit. He was over the moon. He'd be just like his dad, and mum would have to accept it. His mother was distraught when John came home on pre-draft leave, and told her he was going into the war zone. He put his arms round her saying,

'Don't worry Mum, look at Dad, the number of years he has served and fought, he is still going strong. Just believe that I'm happy doing what I'm doing. It's great to be going out there with my mates.'

'Oh John I'm so afraid, just like I am each time your father is deployed to any war zone. I have always had you with me in the past, but now I'll have no one when you are both away.'

'Mum please don't fret. I'll be OK. Remember I have my father's blood in me.'

John's leave ticked on. He went out with his old school pals, and took his mother to the pictures one evening, and the theatre another. He thought she was settling down and accepting the situation. Then the day came that John left to join his unit. Tears were aplenty from his mum. They started to wrench at his heart; he only just managed to keep control. As the front door shut on him his mother stood at the window watching till she could no longer see him.

Ann lay on her bed sobbing her heart out till she fell asleep. When she woke up she went into the shower, letting the water flow over her in an attempt to wash away all her misgivings. While she was drying herself, she made up her mind she would try to get a part-time job to occupy her mind. Luck was on her side. Ann got a nice little job in a local solicitor's office that kept her busy, and filled her time. She was just about settled into her new routine. With neither son nor husband to care for, she made sure to have time to visit her sister. She only lived a little way away so they could have a good old gossip, and went shopping together. She started to be able to enjoy life.

A few weeks later, she had a phone call from husband Dave:

'I'll be home in four days love, so get the kettle on.' She laughed at his usual joke. The day he was due Ann stood in the lounge, adjusting the curtains when she heard a car pull into the drive. *He's early,* she thought, and took another look. Her hand flew to her mouth to stifle the cry. It was what was known as the army "death car". She pulled herself together sufficiently to answer the knock on the door.

'Which one is it?' she managed to say.

'May we come in a minute Mrs James?'

She stood aside proffering her hand to indicate the lounge. Taking a deep breath she followed them in, and sank down onto a chair, still in a daze.

'I'm afraid your husband has been severely injured by an IED, (the b*****d's). He's receiving treatment in the hospital out there to stabilize him for the journey home. Is there anyone we can fetch to be with you?'

'Yes please, my sister lives in the next road.'

One of the officers remained with Ann while the other drove off for her sister. When they came back, and started to pull into the drive they had to brake hard, another “death car” was in there. Ann’s sister Molly gasped out,

‘Oh no, not John as well.’

# The Deserted Barn

Hannah Fox put on her snug red thermal jumper and trousers over her t-shirt and woolly tights. Next she donned her motorbike leathers and boots followed by a headover, her helmet and heated gauntlets. She finally heaved on her rucksack containing sandwiches and a flask. Have I got everything? she thought doing a mental check on her packing. She gave her Kawasaki 600 the once over, checking the security of the panniers containing a smart interview suit and accessories, got on the bike, started the engine and off she went. Hannah had a hundred and eighty mile journey ahead of her to see Kate, a childhood friend, and her husband

Gren. She was so looking forward to seeing her old friend and having a good catch up and gossip.

Kate knew Hannah's lifestyle had completely changed since she'd married. They had been very much country girls, loving their lives in the village they had both grown up in. Life had been so much fun in those days. They used to take part in the local equestrian events on their beloved ponies Bracken and Maple and spent many happy hours hacking in the surrounding countryside. Both girls had been reluctant to grow up, leave school and go to work. They had spent a lot of time discussing this.

'I really don't want to leave school or go to work. I enjoy school life, and the thought of having to give that up to go to work is a torment,' confessed Hannah to her friend.

'Do you know...,' said Kate pondering as she spoke, 'funny you should say that because I'm the same.' She turned and patted her tethered pony.

'I shall feel as though I am deserting dear old Maple.'

'Quite; and the thought of university is abhorrent as well,' Kate replied with a shudder, as she also patted Bracken.

Although intelligent people, neither of them wanted to go to university, so they opted for working in the nearby town. Hannah worked in an accountant's office and Kate as an assistant to the owner of a travel agency. This was how Kate came to meet her husband, Gren. After a whirlwind romance they married a year later. It was a lovely wedding in the village church. Looking round, as they stood waiting in the church porch for the bride to arrive, Hannah was surprised at the number of onlookers standing out on the pavement.

Kate looked beautiful as she walked down the isle on her father's arm, in her softly fitted long white dress with a billowing veil, which flowed to the floor forming a train. Hannah was her only bridesmaid, and she was gorgeous in her dress, which was a flattering, delicate pale green with a flared skirt brushing the floor, and a matching fascinator on her head.

Dan Manton was delighted to be in the congregation. He was a friend of Gren's from a few years back and was over the moon to learn his friend was marrying. He had met Kate a while ago, and had thought she was perfect for Gren. While Dan was admiring Kate as she came gracefully down the isle, his eyes alighted on Hannah. Wow, he had thought, what a stunner! At the reception he plucked up the courage to go over to her.

'Would you like to dance?' he said, holding out his hand.

Hannah looked up with a rather wicked grin saying 'Yes, if you don't mind the fact I'm a hopeless dancer.'

'I'll take my chances on that,' he replied with a chuckle, adding 'I'm probably not much better, so we can tread on each other.'

'On your own head be it,' Hannah said getting up and hooking the hem of her dress to her wrist.

As they danced they found they were very happy in each other's company, sharing the same sense of humour. Hannah was a bit reserved about getting too friendly as she was hoping to move on, extending her career, and to take in more travel. When the evening ended Hannah bid Dan farewell rather reluctantly and left with her parents.

The relationship did continue, but with the proviso from Hannah that she couldn't get serious as she might move on career wise. Dan accepted this, but nurtured the idea that if she moved, maybe he could too. He had strong feelings for her.  And although they never discussed it; Hannah felt the same for him.

A year later Gren heard about a very good travel agency business, which had come on the market in Wensley; a town nearly two hundred miles away.

'Do we or don't we buy it?' said Gren, as he walked round the room in contemplation.

'If you think it will be a good proposition Gren, then we must, but speak to your financial advisor first, please.' Kate said. 'We have to think of the upheaval of leaving family and friends and we won't have my income.'

After much deliberation, Kate and Gren decided it was too good a chance to miss and Gren bought it, so they packed their bags and went, but not before both girls had had a tearful farewell.

'I'm so glad you've got Dan,' Kate said as they hugged each other. He will look out for you.

'That's true although. I don't want it to get too serious. He's a lovely person, I adore him, but

I want to see the world a bit before I settle down.'

Naturally the two girls were upset about the parting, but it was a case of "Que sera sera." Hannah was mortified at the separation, but accepted that she must get on with her own life. They had long since out-grown their ponies, which had been sold. With the proceeds from the sale of her pony, Hannah, much to the concern of her parents and Dan, purchased a motorbike that gave her a lot of pleasure.

Any opportunity the girls got to meet up they took, although this was becoming more and more difficult. Hannah had moved her career on and was employed in marketing for a national company and was subsequently travelling abroad quite often. Dan was getting edgy because of the amount of time she was away. He knew he had to accept this, as it was part of Hannah. But he wanted her to know how much he missed her.

'Hannah I do know; and appreciate you have to travel for your job. I will never try to stop you. I think too much of you for that. My main worry is that..., do you realize how much I miss you?'

'I have a pretty good idea Dan. I hope you know I miss you too, but my absences are unavoidably part of my job. I wish it could be different, but it isn't and we must make the best of it,' Hannah replied with a heavy heart. She felt more for Dan than she had wanted to.

'I can cope Hannah, as long as I know you feel the same,' Dan said, with great relief.

Kate had become pregnant early into their marriage; she and Gren had a gorgeous baby son called Oliver who was the joy of their lives. Happy as she was with motherhood she was having difficulties coping with the baby and working demanding hours with her husband in their agency. Gren could see how stressed Kate was becoming. This was added to by the increase of business.

'What do you think of the idea if I asked Hannah whether she would consider working in the business?' he asked his wife one evening when the strain was really telling on her. Kate looked up in amazement... 'That would be great,' she responded, 'but let me make the call please.'

Kate phoned Hannah, 'I wondered whether you would like to come down for a few days, and have a chat with Gren? He needs some help with the business, and thought it would be the right job for you. Trade has increased faster than we had expected. It is now too much for me along with the baby. Knowing you as I do; I think it's the perfect situation for you. Come down and have a chat, eh?'

Hannah couldn't miss the longing in Kate's voice.

'Kate, it would be lovely to come and see you all. I like the idea of a working with Gren. He's such a nice bloke and very dedicated to his work. Funnily enough I've been thinking of changing my job again. I'll speak to my boss regarding some holiday, and let you know if, and when.'

Reflecting on Hannah's response, Gren was sure the position would suit Hannah. She was a very presentable young lady in her mid twenties; she was medium height, slimly built and had a head of delightful blonde curls. She had good business acumen, and had travelled a fair amount; ideal for the position Gren needed to fill quickly since the advent of their baby. Needless to say, Hannah had to do a lot of soul searching, regarding her relationship with Dan. In the end her attitude was that she really wanted the job that Gren offered, and hoped she would qualify for it. Her CV read well so she was hopeful.

Having prepared for the journey, it wasn't as straightforward as Hannah had anticipated. The weather had started out being promising, but was now turning very cold and grey with the bikers dread of a strong wind. She had covered nearly a hundred miles when, to her relief, the wind dropped; then the curse of fog was forming and she realised she had taken the wrong road as a result.

'Oh shit!' she said in exasperation. 'Where the hell am I?'

She travelled on a little further hoping to find a road sign, but no chance. Eventually she saw a shape through the now dense fog, and proceeded carefully to discover it looked like a small farm, so she gingerly rode into the muddy yard. There was no sign of light, life or even an animal.

Feeling a little bewildered and nervous, she got off her bike, and walked over to what appeared to be a barn. She struggled to heave open the huge unlocked door which creaked and groaned in protest. She wrinkled up her nose at the putrid smell that invaded her nostrils; *probably stale manure or damp hay,* she thought.

'Blast! It's too dark,' she exclaimed. 'I'll have to get my torch. I'm pretty sure this place is deserted, but at least I can sort out my map and find how to get back on the right road,' she muttered, not feeling at all happy with the situation she was in. 'This damn fog has really messed me up.'

Having got her torch, Hannah went back into the barn absolutely cringing at the smell, which was still strong even though she had left the door open.

As she shone her torch around the barn, Hannah froze in sheer horror. Was she seeing things? She rubbed her eyes. Then refocused on the beam of light. No she was imagining it. Her torch had picked up what appeared to be a body that had started to decay. It was hanging from a beam. She let out a horrendous scream and pressed her hand to her mouth as she raced out of the barn, retching and feeling faint with shock, and her mind went blank. For a long while she couldn't think what to do. She couldn't just leave the body, but she couldn't go back in there.

After a while, Hannah began to feel a little better and realised she must call the emergency services.

'Oh! I don't bloody believe it,' she shouted in exasperation when she realised she had no reception on her mobile. 'I'll have to ride up the lane till I get a signal. I'm not feeling good at all, but it has to be done.'

With great effort she pulled herself together and got on her bike. Hannah finally picked up a signal at the top of the lane and dialed 999. She didn't know the name of the lane or the farm to tell them so the police asked her to stay where she was so that they could find her. They finally arrived along with an ambulance and a doctor. Hannah couldn't face going into the barn again. A police officer stayed with her and took a statement.

The medical officer confirmed the body to be that of a middle aged man with the build of a working farmer. The corpse was removed.

'I want the barn searched thoroughly,' Sergeant Cole ordered his men, but it showed no sign of a struggle. 'OK, so that shows nothing. I'm beginning to strongly suspect that it could be a suicide.' He then directed his men to search the cottage.

The police turned the cottage over, desperate to find evidence as to the cause of the obvious suicide.

'Would you like to come inside out of the damp weather Miss?'

'I don't really want to, but it is wet and cold out here.'

She submitted feeling very uneasy, but went in. A Woman Police Officer made her a cup of tea, which had to be black as there was no milk, but had plenty of sugar in it. While sitting there she looked around and she could see that the cottage had once been a cared for, comfortable home. Lots of chintz, well polished brown furniture, and plenty of loved ornaments, though it clearly hadn't been looked after recently. Hannah noticed that what had once been well polished cared for floorboards were now neglected.

'Look!' she called to the police. 'Where one of the rugs have slipped the boards are scuffed at the end of two of them.'

She had sat almost idly wondering why they were so scuffed then realised they could be access to something hidden below. Going over to where Hannah pointed. One of the officers squatted down to take a closer look.

'You're right Miss, they have been taken up a lot,' he said. Rubbing his chin in contemplation.

'I'll just go and find a jemmy and get them up. I think there is something suspicious here.' Having got the boards up he called the sergeant over.

'Uhaa,' uttered the sergeant, 'what have we here then?

Underneath there was enough room to stand. Two officers went down to inspect the area. One came back with a look of satisfaction on his face.

'Sarge!' He called. Sergeant Cole went over. 'Look Sarge,' and held up a bag of powder. 'This is just a small example of what's down here, you must come down and see.'

Sergeant Cole descended the steps, and was as amazed as the two constables.

'This is not our job. I must call in the drug squad,' he said feeling pleased to have some lead as to the hanging. 'Come up you two; we'll let the drug squad deal with this now. I must say a very big thanks to you, Miss, for your observations.'

Hannah had been as surprised as the rest about the developments, but was getting anxious as the time was getting on. She still had a number of miles to cover.

'Can I leave now? I still have a good distance to go.'

'I'm afraid not yet. I have to ask you to wait until the drug squad has come and they will decide what will happen,' replied Sergeant Cole.

When the drug squad arrived they went straight down into the cellar, and found a bench with carefully measured bags of cocaine. Sergeant Mason, the drugs officer, turned to his men.

'I am certain this has been cut with something.'

'I agree sir,' replied one officer.

'I want tests done on all of it, to be sure,' the Sergeant instructed.

They carried out a quick test, and confirmed it was not of marketable quality. It would be put through more stringent tests back at the laboratory.

'Right, so that would clearly pose a big problem for any drug dealer,' Sergeant Mason told everyone.

'We need to get busy interviewing the surrounding neighbours to find out more about the farmer,' Sergeant Cole, and Sergeant Mason instructed their men.

After interviewing the neighbours, the police discovered the deceased farmer, Noel Jackson, had appeared to change from a pleasant person to a very surly one. Neighbours knew the farm was not doing well, and there had been strangers calling there. It also turned out that Mrs. Jackson had walked out roughly a year ago, which was a shame; she was a nice homely person who did a lot of good work in the village. No one seemed to know what made her leave.

Sergeant Mason managed to locate Mrs. Jackson who was living in a flat in a nearby town. When she opened the door her face was a picture of concern.

'Mrs. Jackson, may I come in please? I have some rather bad news for you.'

Her hand flew to her face; her mouth opened, but no words came. She turned to signal the Sergeant into the flat, and in the habitual way offered him a cup of tea.

'No thank you Mrs. Jackson,' replied Mason as he took a seat. 'Please sit down while I tell you the happenings.' Mrs. Jackson squatted on the edge of a chair, as if ready to spring off.

'I'm afraid I have to inform you that your husband appears to have committed suicide...Mrs. Jackson.'

She let out a squeal, and buried her head in her hands. After a short time she raised her head, and spoke in an abnormally calm voice.

'How did he do that then Sergeant?'

Sergeant Mason told her as gently as he could.

'Aaah,' she said. 'That confirms the suspicions I've had for a long while. I'm sure he was being threatened, but he ignored this. He was desperate to get money to clear the farm debts. He always said if he could do that he would finish with the whole business. But I'm not so sure that would have been the case. I'm sure he was in with a bad crowd, but he would never talk about any of it.'

At the end of his meeting Sergeant Mason was certain he had left a very distressed lady who was trying to put the past behind her. She was distraught when she heard of her husband's suicide.

'Shall I get someone to stay with you?'

'No Sergeant, I shall be alright. But thank you.'

A further extended search of the cottage, farm buildings, and other out buildings was organised by Sergeant Mason. Each area was completely turned over. There was a loud whoop of excitement when the drug squad and their officers eventually found a carefully concealed large hole in an out building. Boards had been put over the hole with earth on top, and then a piece of farm machinery placed over that. When they took off the boards they could hardly believe their eyes. There was a large cache of illegal guns. At this stage of the operation the Met were called in along with the firearms unit and forensics. It would appear that the drugs operation was a cover up for a very lucrative gun running business. Fire Arms and Forensics did a further search; this was proving bigger than first thought. Sergeant Cole confided in Sergeant Mason:

'I'm not surprised that Mr. Jackson found it all too much. And I think his wife was on the right track.'

There was a full scale stake-out set up at the farm by both the Met and the drug squad. The sergeants of both units were urgent in their bidding as time was short.

'Sergeants -- you, you and you, take a couple of constables with you and secrete yourselves at the back door ready to seize them if they come that way,' were Detective Chief Inspector Langton's orders.

Firstly a van arrived, and three aggressive looking men got out.

'Go round the rear to the back door quietly, let yourselves in and wait for us to come in at the front. I don't think there is anyone there, but keep your eyes and ears open.'

This came from a thick set, rough looking man, speaking as he pulled a balaclava over his head.

'The rest of you come with me to the front.'

The hooded men entered the back door stealthily. The hidden police sprang into action. After an initial wild struggle from the criminals, with attempts to shout warnings to their colleagues; the officers, in a very quiet and swift fashion, seized them. They were handcuffed and bundled outside into a camouflaged vehicle. They were supervised while the stakeout continued. Finally the gunrunners arrived, and made straight for the cottage expecting to be met by the drug dealers. The Met police were waiting, but kept hidden and quiet. The gunrunner's leader looked around for the drug dealers.

'Where the bloody hell are they?' he shouted to the other men, in an ugly tone. 'I don't like the look of this...'

'No boss something's not right. Let's get out of here!'

'What! After all the trouble I've been to? Get real man! We're here to complete a job and that's what will happen. Right you lot. Get yourselves sorted. We're going in.'

'That's what I like to hear,' said DCI Langton, with a chuckle to his sergeant, 'a nice decisive person who doesn't let me down. Are we ready then?'

The sergeant gave a brief look at his men, and gave a thumbs up and nod to his boss.

When the door burst open, the men stood there gobsmacked.

'Get 'em lads,' urged the DCI.

'What's all this? I 'aven't done nufink, I just come to visit my friend,' whinged one of the men as he cringed into a corner.

'Sorry mate. You'll have the chance to prove that at the nick,' said the Sergeant as he handcuffed him.

'I've only come to collect what's mine,' the leader of the gang growled.

Twisting and turning he became ugly, trying to kick his captors 'gerrof you stupid man, I ain't done nufink wrong. I left some belongings here and I want them back,' he said, as he carried on fighting to get free.

'And what would that be sir?' asked the DCI, with a metaphoric tongue in his cheek. 'I think you have a lot to answer for, and even more if you don't stop struggling,' he said, getting impatient with the man. 'There is a man so distraught that he appears to have hung himself. And a heartbroken wife left. That is all on top of the lives you ruin with drugs, and those that are taken by your guns. There is only one place for you, my man, and that has bar's on it.'

There was intense dislike in Langton's voice.

A lot of struggling and pleading of innocence continued from the men, but all to no avail. The police had enough evidence and fingerprints to prove their guilt; they would be in court the next day. The outcome was that the drugs Noel Jackson had been buying to sell on had been cheap; unwittingly he had thought the drugs were a bargain. He hadn't realised how he was being conned into being a cover up. He had lost the last of his money when it wouldn't sell, and was then being blackmailed because of the gun running. His actions were those of a desperate man; a man to be pitied if it hadn't been for the poor people whose dreadful habit he had assisted.

Hannah had badly wanted to stay to see the results, but had to continue her journey as the job interview was urgent. The police assured her she would be notified of the outcome.

'DCI Langton said you can get off Miss,' said the kindly WPC, 'The DCI says he will be in touch. You may be called as a witness.'

She eventually arrived at Kate's house for a quick wash and change.

'I'll tell you all about it later, but I must get a quick wash and brush up, and go to see Gren,' Hannah said, giving her friend a hug and kiss.

When she got to Gren's office just before they locked up, she was a bit out of breath, but said:

'I must tell you what happened to me on my journey here. The fog came down and I lost my way. I ended up in an old deserted farm, and well – you will hardly believe me when I tell you all that happened, which includes a body hanging from a barn roof, drugs under the cottage floorboards, and guns in the outhouses. A real racket was being run from there.'

Gren stood there with his mouth dropping open and his eyes staring at her in disbelief.

'No! You're making it up.' He said, not quite taking it in. 'Now come on, admit it you simply got lost, and it took you a long while to find the right road again.'

'You're wrong Gren. I almost wish you were right, but what I told you is absolutely true.'

'Oh my God! Then sit down and I'll get Sally to make you a cup of tea, you poor thing.'

He sat her down in a comfortable chair and explained the job to her. He told her:

'It will involve a busy life, and you would have to travel abroad quite often inspecting hotels and speaking with clients from time to time. There will be a lot of interaction with staff and holidaymakers. What do you think you could put into the job?' he asked as he scrutinized her reaction to what he had said.

'I could put in a lot of knowledge from having travelled before, but I think the best thing would be a passion for the job and the love of seeing satisfied customers,' was her decisive reply. After a pause and a sip of her tea, she continued: 'I have a lot to offer the post; my travels have been fairly extensive, and I have studied a large variety of countries. It's given me a wide idea of good areas for holidays.'

She was very taken with the sound of the position, and longed to be deemed right for it. She gave Gren her CV and waited, hardly able to breathe while Gren perused it. She really wanted this job. He folded it, passed it back to her, shook her hand, and offered her a very lucrative package. Hannah was in seventh heaven! After her experience earlier she couldn't believe her luck.

Arriving back at Kate's, she realized she hadn't phoned her parents or Dan. She asked Kate if she could use her phone.

'Of course you can,' said Kate with a rather secretive look, which puzzled Hannah.

'Come and see me in the kitchen before you phone Dan,'

When she had finished relating her story to her mum, Kate went to find her friend in the kitchen. Opening the door she stood there gawping, not able to believe her eyes. There sat Dan looking at her with an expression of love on his face.

'Hello darling. You didn't expect to see me did you?' as he walked over to her with his arms open wide.

'Dan! Wow, this is lovely, but... how? Did you know he was coming Kate?'

'Yes of course I did! I picked up from your voice that he meant a lot to you, and your mother confirmed it, so there you are.'

Hannah moved quickly into Dan's waiting arms, and Kate crept out of the room leaving them to it.

The police eventually let Hannah know that they had a very successful outcome, closing what had been a large and successful operation. Those who had perpetrated the crimes were now behind bars serving stiff sentences. She received an invite to a special awards evening. She was presented with a medal for her part in the discovery of the setup.

# My Favourite Gentleman

Each morning Agnes listened for the sound of his shuffling footsteps, knowing they were bringing him closer. This morning, as any other, she would take up her usual position. Which was in the comfortable old-fashion chintz chair in the bay window with faded curtains that matched the chair. From here she could watch the changing of the seasons, as well as listen for Walter. Easing her stiff old body into the chair, she adjusted the elegant tasselled cushion to support her back. She relaxed knowing how well she was able to hear his arrival.

This spring morning she could see the trees starting to take on a delicate shade of green as the buds were opening, and the daffodils buds burgeoning with the merest sign of yellow at the tips. *Walter will be so happy to see this after all the snow,* she thought smiling to herself. *Aah that's him coming now.* His white hair and bushy beard made up for the lack of snow. His regular staff clutched in one hand making sure he could walk safely, and the other holding a bag of some sort. *I wonder what that's for,* Agnes mused. She reached up and flung open the window in anticipation as Walter got closer.

'Good morning Walter!' she called. 'How are you today? Are your bones easier in this sunny weather?'

'Indeed they are Agnes. Kind of you to enquire. Have you got the kettle on?'

'I certainly have my good man.'

Walter opened the cottage door and wiped his feet. He lodged his staff against the coat stand and discarded his faithful old trench coat, but kept a close hold on the bag.

'Here you are old man; a good hot cup of tea. 'Twill warm the cockles of your heart. Why are you holding onto that bag?'

'That's for me to know, and you to find out my dear,' replied Walter as he took a large swig of his tea. Agnes spotted the glimmer of a smile on his face, and knew he was teasing her.

What Agnes didn't know was that Walter, while on his ramble, had come across a pretty, but wild cat who had just had a litter of kittens. His observations had told him she wasn't able to look after them properly. He had made up his mind he would provide them with some extra warmth, thus the straw he was carrying in his bag. He was hoping to make her a bit more of a bed, adding to her warmth. This would give the mother a little more time to feed the kittens before he tried to find homes for them.

When Walter had drunk his tea he explained to Agnes,

'While I was on one of my rambles I came across a pretty, but wild cat who had just had a litter of kittens.'

'How lovely,' said Agnes, a warm gentle smile on her face.

'It would be if she was able to look after them properly. I have been watching them and she isn't up to the job. Could be that she is too young herself.'

'What a shame. Is there anything we can do for them,' Agnes asked, her smile disappearing.

'Well now my dear, that's what I've got here in my bag. I was going to tell you, you nosey old thing, when I had drunk my tea, but no you couldn't wait could you?' Walter said with a chuckle.

'You stop you're cheek my good man or you'll have a taste of my hand,' she said, her chuckle joining his.

Agnes was surprised at his revelations, but understood his thinking. She looked around the big old kitchen, where they sat drinking their tea. While she did she took in the old range, and the ceiling to floor cupboards on either side. This made her aware of the warmth in the room.

'If I emptied out one of these cupboards it could be used as a bed. It would do for two of the kittens, and I would love the company,' she said, looking at the old man waiting for his opinion.

After a few moments pondering, Walter grunted. She was sure it was a grunt of approval, but didn't like to push.

'Do you know woman, that's a good idea of yours. I'm fairly certain I can find homes for three of them, but I would have been stuck for the other two.'

'We will go and collect them next week when they've had the chance to benefit from this bedding, and I don't think it will be too soon by the look of the mother; she's had enough.'

When the elderly pair got to the home of the cats they were mortified. There was no sign of the mother cat and all but one of the kittens were dead.

Walter's language was none too polite when he saw the decimation before him; Agnes was in tears. It was pretty obvious that this was a vicious attack by human beings; not predation.

'I saw those little buggers messing about in these woods. I had a feeling they were up to no good, but truth be known I was scared to say anything in case they set about me. What a coward I am, I could've probably saved these poor little things.'

'Now don't take on so Walter!  You're right. They may well have set about you, and left you lying here injured. It could have been days before anyone had known.'

The words were no sooner out of her mouth than she fell to the ground in a heap. Hearing the thud as she hit the ground, and the simultaneous murderous yell from a bunch of four youths, Walter spun round from where he had been looking for the remaining kitten. He couldn't believe his eyes as he took in what was happening. The next thing he knew, he was seeing a hefty lump of wood coming at speed to his head. He attempted to shield it off with his arms, but it was too quick. His head was split open with the force of the blow. His body crumpled, and he was lying in a pool of blood.

The tiny little kitten that had survived the attack was shaking with the cold. It had crawled out of its hiding place, and detected the warmth from Agnes' body. He snuggled up to her, his rough little tongue licking her face. This made Agnes stir. She rubbed her face where she thought it was tickling, and in doing so her hand touched the fur of the kitten's face. A few minutes later she started to regain consciousness. Looking about her she could just make out Walters form on the ground. Eventually she was able to sit up. The kitten was pressing close to her, unwilling to lose the warmth it had found.

'Walter?' She called as loudly as she could. 'Walter, can you hear me?' Still no reply. Looking around in anguish Agnes was desperate, what could she do? Her eyes caught sight of a stick and she realised it was Walters. By shifting her bottom bit by bit she was able to reach it. Having grasped the stick, Agnes could just reach far enough with it to give Walter a poke. She did this twice, and on the second prod, he stirred.

'Wake up Walter!' Agnes shouted. 'Wake up! We've got to get out of here. Oh My God!'

Agnes had spotted Walters head injury. She knew he would never be able to get up and walk. Her body sagged as she buried her head in her hands. *How on earth can I manage this now?* The little kitten meowed to remind her he was still there.

'Oh you poor little thing. I must get you back, and warm too, but Walter has to be my priority. Please God give me the strength to get up and walk.'

With that, Agnes gathered herself together, mustering every ounce of strength she could. And with the aid of Walter's staff she hauled her body up, standing still for a few minutes to let her body get used to being upright. She then bent and picked up the kitten, tucking it into her coat pocket. With a few painful grunts and groans Agnes got her legs to work, steadily putting one in front of the other. She was beginning to feel as if she wasn't going to make it when she saw the road a few steps away. She stopped for breath before making the mammoth effort to take the final steps. Standing in the road praying a vehicle would appear she put her hand into her pocket, and stroked the kitten in reassurance. A van came in to view. Agnes waved the staff, and her arm out to stop it. When it came to a halt the driver got out.

'Agnes what *are* you doing?' Squinting her eyes as she looked up to focus on the mans face she let out a half sob,

'Rob, it's you!' She exclaimed almost falling against him. He was her good friend's son. She quickly told him of the events. Rob was staggered that this could happen in a quiet little village like this.

'Now Agnes, you get in the van and wait while I go and find Walter. Don't worry. Lock yourself in, and nurse that kitten to help it get properly warm. I won't be long.'

Agnes sat there stroking the kitten, and while doing so she decided to call it Monty. She didn't know why; she just liked the name, and thought it suited him. This decided, her head drooped as she gradually drifted off to sleep. She woke up with a jump when Rob gently tapped the window. She came too with difficulty. Then she suddenly became aware Rob had Walter draped round him. He looked in a bad way.

'Oh dear oh lor Rob, let me help you.'

'No Agnes. Please just sit still. You are injured too don't forget. I can manage. I'll soon have the poor old fella sorted.'

Rob opened the back door of the van, and with a struggle he managed to get Walter in. He sat him up leaning him against the side of the van, and held him there with the straps he used to secure cargo with. Getting into the drivers seat Rob said to Agnes,

'Agnes I'm taking you both to hospital. I think you saw that Walter is in a bad way, and needs expert attention, and you need to be checked over. The kitten will be fine in a box I have got in the back.'

Agnes was about to protest, but as she tried to get out of the van her head started to swim.

'All right Rob; I'll do as I'm told.

Walter was kept in hospital for a few days. Rob drove Agnes home with the kitten. She put it in the cupboard next to the range with the door wide open, and food and milk just in front. At the end of the week there was a tap on the door. Agnes opened it, and Rob greeted her with,

'Hello Agnes, I thought you would like to know Walter is being discharged, but only if he is he not left on his own.'

'Come in lad, come in. Now what's this all about? Walter can only come out of hospital if he goes somewhere to be looked after…is that right?'

'In a nutshell, yes Agnes.'

'Well what are you waiting for boy. Fetch him here. I have a nice room for him, and would be happy looking after the old so and so. You go and get him, and don't stand any nonsense from him. He's to come here, and that's that.'

'Do you know, I thought you would say that Agnes. You are a lovely pair of old codgers. You were made for each other. See you later. Bye. '

# Bluebell Cottage

Grabbing her coat and calling Bentley, her faithful spaniel, she put his lead on. Gemma had to get out of the house, with all its sad memories that swamped her. *Walk, walk,* she told herself, *clear your head.* As she tramped down the lane, with the mud squelching beneath her boots it lent satisfaction to her sore heart. Bentley had charged ahead, but kept running back as though making sure she was alright. Gemma could gradually feel her head clearing. She was starting to focus properly on the recent happenings.

Ed had left her. This time it was final, fineto, finished. The letter left on her bureau said it all.

She knew that her life had to be put back together. She recalled their last conversation:

'You should've bloody well known the situation before we married Gemma. Why didn't you get yourself checked, knowing how much I wanted children,' Ed shouted as he stomped about the room.

'I had no reason to suspect there would be any problem. How many women do? If you were so fussed, why didn't you suggest I had a check-up?' Gemma stormed back.

Ed glared at her with a look of absolute fury, and with dislike on his face. Turning his back on her, he retorted. 'It's not my job to instruct you with the basics of life and what to expect from marriage.'

'Well now I know what not to expect, that's for sure. Perhaps you are not mature enough to realise a little support wouldn't go amiss under the circumstances...'

Before the end of her sentence had reached him, she heard a resounding thud followed by footsteps on the concrete.

Her arms wrapping around herself in a hug, her body bent over as she mourned the space where her dysfunctional womb had been. There were no more tears left to be cried. Ed had been his usual heartless self. He, like her, had desperately wanted a child. Now that could no longer happen. The doctors had had to perform a hysterectomy after the last miscarriage. Now she had nothing. No baby, no husband, and no womb.

'Why does all this have to happen to me?' she wailed in a loud voice.

She sank down onto a rock. Bentley's nose nuzzled her. Finally, she rose and started to walk again. She turned right down a lane she had never been down before. After a couple of miles the lane turned into a track. Curiosity got the better of her. She felt the urge to keep walking.

Gemma saw a turning on the left. She decided to follow this. The turning went in a half circle. She stopped when she spotted, behind many bushes, a cottage. She was hesitant to go closer, having a desire to not appear nosey. Gemma walked along in front of it as casually as she could. Arriving at the gate, she ventured a side ways glance at the building. There were curtains at the windows that were all closed. There seemed to be an unlived-in appearance to the cottage. *Such a shame* she thought, as a chocolate box lid came to mind. *It is lovely, the sort of place you could disappear into and live quietly. Without being bothered.*

Gemma whistled for Bentley, who was busy trying to dig through a rabbit burrow. He reproachfully looked up, and as she pointed her finger to the ground next to her, he begrudgingly went to her side. She stood at the gate for quite a few minutes, trying to work out whether the cottage was inhabited or not. Her question was answered when the dog snuck away down the path to the front door. He pushed it with his nose, and the door opened. Gemma was alarmed. She expected to hear a shout of anger at the intrusion, but none came. Realising Bentley had gone in she hurried to the door, and peered round it.

'Hello, is anyone there? I'm sorry my dog has invited himself in.'

When there was no reply she went in further feeling very awkward about taking liberties. On seeing Bentley's black tail wagging from behind a chair Gemma ventured over to see why. When she reached the chair, Bentley started to paw the carpet and whine. Looking down, she drew her breath in sharply. Her eyes focused on the form of an elderly woman lying inert on the floor. Dragging the dog away, and making him sit, she touched the woman's neck. Yes, there was a pulse, all be it weak, but she daren't move her.

Looking around for a telephone she spotted one on the dresser, quickly dialing emergency, requesting the police and ambulance.

'Now what shall we do Bentley? We really can't go and leave her like this.' Bentley gave his answer by making himself comfortable next to the woman.

Half an hour later, Gemma started to pace the floor. She had put a cushion under the ladies head and gone upstairs to fetch a blanket to wrap around her.

'If they are much longer I will need to get some information from a doctor as to what to do.'

This was said to a very interested Bentley whose head was tipping from side to side as he listened. It occurred to Gemma she should look for something to identify the woman, and whether there was anyone she could contact. Luckily she found an envelope addressed to her that showed her as being Mrs. Maine.

Just as she was putting the envelope back, Gemma knocked a knob that made a concealed draw open. She was about to close it when curiosity got the better of her. Thinking it might contain a contact for the old lady, it made Gemma feel less guilty for looking, but she got the surprise of her life when some photos slipped out of a fold of paper. They were very old sepia photos showing Mrs. Maine as a beautiful young lady. On delving further, Gemma found newspaper cuttings depicting the young lady in various dramas. A further paper advertised a film she had starred in.

'Oh my goodness, she was famous. What ever happened to her to make her shut herself away here?'

Gemma again found herself talking to Bentley as she would a person, only this time he ignored her. His job of guarding the old lady was far more important.

Gemma had tried to talk with Mrs. Maine again, but the poor lady was so confused she made no sense. In the end she replaced all the pictures and cuttings. She would have to spend some time with Mrs. Maine when she was compos mentos.

'Ah! Here are the police and ambulance at last.'

Running to open the door, and holding on to the dog at the same time, she pointed to Mrs Maine, telling them her name. The police were busy going through her desk trying to get some information.

'Well Madam, it would initially appear to have been a robbery. We have contacted the local vicar. He has informed us that Mrs Maine's gardener had started work with a digger to create a pond for her. While doing this he came across what appeared to be pieces of large stone which clearly weren't ordinary garden rocks or stones. Oh dear, I'm not too sure I should be telling you all this,' said the flustered policeman.

'Please do officer. I shan't spread any chitchat. I'm more concerned about Mrs. Maine.'

'Well,' he continued, 'the vicar called in a local historian for Mrs. Maine. And it would appear it's all the remains of an ancient burial plot which, it's fairly certain, contains some valuables that in those days were buried with the bodies. Excavation is due to take place shortly. Whoever did this to the poor old girl has tried, unsuccessfully, to dig some up for their own gains.'

'How heartless can people be? This dear lady has done nothing to deserve this. I must see what the situation is with her. Is she badly injured?'

'I don't know yet. Whoever they were, they were quite brutal with her,' the officer said.

The paramedics where working on Mrs Maine, who was beginning to look a little more with it. She looked expectantly at Gemma.

'Who are you? Do I know you?'

'No you don't,' Mrs. Maine I'm...'

'This is the good lady who found you and phoned for us. Her name is Gemma,' the paramedic told her.

'Oh my goodness, thank you dear very much, now you go into the kitchen, and make yourself a nice cup of tea, and you'll find some biscuits in the cupboard. Just help yourself.'

The paramedic turned to Gemma.

We are taking her into hospital; it will probably be an overnight stay. We've patched her up pretty well, but she needs some proper stiches on a couple of wounds. The rest is bad bruising. Taking in to consideration her age, she should be in for observation.'

'What about the house? The lock has been damaged,' said Gemma

'That's alright miss, I've got a man coming to replace it,' replied the policeman.

Gemma went over to the ambulance as they were putting the patient in. She took hold of her hand, and assured her she would come and see her the next day. The officer came to them as Gemma was leaving the ambulance.

'Mrs. Maine has asked if you would stay here for the night and if possible until she gets home?' he said. 'She has no near relatives and is worried about her treasures.'

'Of course I will, so long as she doesn't mind my dog. There are some tit-bits I can give him and I have nothing to hurry home for. I am quite willing to stay here.'

Mrs Maine heard this, and her face lit up at the prospect. 'How lovely to have you and your lovely dog as guests.'

As Gemma lay in bed that night, she was in deep thought. How she would love to live here in this lovely cottage. Her mind was plunged into random thoughts, I *could sell the house which Ed has left me, and live on the proceeds, or buy this cottage from Mrs. Maine, who could still live here. Oh yes? I would love to have someone to look after.* All these thoughts drifted around her mind until she fell into a deep sleep that didn't include Ed.

What she hadn't done was to cater for Ed's selfishness and greed. Two weeks later Gemma was still at Mrs. Maine's home. The dear lady had begged Gemma to remain living with her. The cottage was large enough to allow her her own space, and the old lady loved Bentley. They had been settled in for three weeks when there was a knock on the door. Skipping over to answer it, Gemma stood there for a second, then she rubbed her eyes, thinking she was seeing things. When she realised she wasn't, she tried to slam the door shut, but he put his foot in to stop her. There stood Ed!

'Go away! I never want to see you again,' Gemma shouted as she tried to force the door closed.

'Now now, temper, temper,' he said in a smarmy voice. 'I need to speak to you about our house.'

'Our house? What on earth do you mean? You said I was to have it,' Gemma said, appalled at what he implied.

'That was then, this is now. I need my share from it,' Ed replied

'No, you go and see a solicitor. I have it in writing from you that it is mine; your signature is on the note. So push off and forget it,' responded Gemma, getting very heated.

With that she caught Ed unaware and slammed the door shut. Going back into Mrs. Maine and Bentley, she explained roughly what had happened. Mrs. Maine was furious.

'Let him have it my dear, you don't need it. You have this place. I'm getting my solicitor to come here, and with your sanction I'm signing the house over to you. No! Don't argue, now be a good girl and make us a nice cup of tea. While we drink it there are some things I want to tell you.'

Mrs. Maine proceeded with the story of her life and how she came to live here.

'In my younger days I was a famous actress, Yolande Harte. I married a wonderful man who was also my agent. I was never short of work. James and I bought this cottage as a retreat. We loved it, and had some wonderful times here. It was our sanctuary. Then twenty-five years ago James had a massive heart attack, and died instantly. I didn't know what to do with myself. I very nearly went to pieces, but thank goodness the love James had given me helped me to hold myself together. The only problem was that I couldn't bring myself to work after that, so I sold up all my other properties and came to live here where we had always been so happy. It was the best thing I could have done. Ah,' she said, a dreamy look of reminiscence on her face, 'those wonderful days.' Yolande broke from her reverie and looked at Gemma, 'Life was a bowl of the proverbial cherries. A handsome doting husband, a career I loved. What more could I want? Then bang! It all stopped.'

Yolanda's eyes closed, her face paled. It frightened Gemma. She felt her pulse and that was as normal, so she got a rug and covered her. Mrs. Maine had obviously exhausted herself with all the talk and recalling the past. Gemma collected the tea things and crept into the kitchen with Bentley and left the dear old lady to sleep.

On waking she looked around slightly dazed, then a look of contentment came onto her face when she saw Gemma sitting quietly reading with Bentley curled up on the mat.

'My goodness I must have needed that sleep, I feel totally refreshed. Now... what was I saying before I launched into my life story? Oh yes, Gemma firstly please call me Yolande, and secondly please say you will take the cottage over. You and Bentley have made me happier than I have been since James' death.'

An expression of devotion was clear to see on Gemma's face as she walked over to the dear lady.

'I would love to Yolande. It's amazing I have often had dreams about this place. Thank you so much,' Gemma said with a big lump in her throat.

Yolanda's solicitor arrived the next day. Gemma opened the door to him, and her heart did a summersault. There stood her, and nearly every female's, dream man. A tall, dark, and handsome man. All of a fluster she showed him into Yolande, and as the business took place; Gemma could feel the draw between them.

Business done, Brendan packed his briefcase to leave. Yolande could sense the vibes between them, and had a little chuckle to herself. At the, door Brendan put his hand out to Gemma, and his eyes locked onto hers. He held her hand far longer than necessary, and seemed reluctant to leave. As she closed the door Gemma did a twirl of excitement. She was certain that this was the start of something good.

# The Hapless Girl

The impoverished area of the town was dull in appearance at any time. Shops had no sparkle to their window displays, and paint was peeling off the frames. Pavements collected rubbish, with road surfaces leaving a lot to be desired. All this was emphasised by the continual rain, and never more so than with the miserable morning light attempting to filter through the narrow window of the attic flat bedroom that was above the greengrocers shop.

Here in the attic flat, Alice woke from her fitful slumber in the tiny bedroom she shared with her sister. She lay in her apology of a bed. It had a mattress that was lumpy and hard. The cover stained and full of holes; she used these to stuff the sparse filling back in the vain hope of retaining some flocking in the rotten thing. She stretched to loosen her stiff bones, twisting and turning to get her body working. She welcomed the thought of getting up to go to work in a warm office. The damp and severe chill had worked its evil way on her bones, despite her youth.

As usual, in her discomfort, she would reminisce about life as it used to be. Drifting off to a place of calm and aching familiarity. A lovely home, and a comfortable bed that invited her to stay there in its warmth and cosiness. Before her dear mother came, and gently woke her. She would shower and dress in her school uniform that comprised of a smart white blouse, navy gymslip, blazer and felt brimmed hat, ready for a delicious and nourishing breakfast. Then her father drove her and her sister to their private school in his luxury car. Yes, life had been so very different. Alice was still in full time education.

She was an attractively featured girl with curly straw-coloured hair, blue eyes, and possessor of a delightful figure. Now she had to take care of her little sister, and get her off to school on a very meagre breakfast that was all they could afford and tend to her father who was now disabled. In all, do everything she could to take her dead mother's place.

Alice had never visualised that such a drastic change in life would ever take place, but it did so, and in no uncertain terms; it all started when her adored mother succumbed to the dreaded cancer. Her sister Julie had only been nine years old.Their father, totally devastated, had begun to drink, endeavouring to block the pain of his darling wife's death. This had led to him be responsible for a nearly fatal car crash while under the influence of drink. He had lost control of his car and hit an oncoming one in which two people had died. He suffered severe back injuries. This disabled him from the waist down, confining him to a bed or chair.

Fred's employment was as a director of a flourishing company. He earned a high salary, enabling him to make sure his family lived in an extremely comfortable style. This terminated promptly. During the next few years, their savings and investments dwindled along with their luxurious life style. As time progressed with no income, her father descended into a deep depression. Alice had to take charge of their lives. They had virtually been turned out onto the street through the inability to pay the mortgage. She managed to find a small flat for the three of them. She furnished it with the barest of necessities, and had been able to get a paper round to supplement their now meagre income. She left school at the earliest opportunity so she could work full time to support her father and sister. Touting the streets and agencies she finally found employment in a local office as general factotum, and retained her paper round.

Flushed and weary from delivering the newspapers that were extremely heavy, Alice returned from her round got Julie off to school, and then with a practised hand attended to her father, dressing him in his shirt, fair-isle pullover, tweed jacket, and grey flannels; all of which had seen better days. She accepted the verbal abuse thrown at her from the disagreeable man who she could hardly recognise any longer. She gave him his scant breakfast, then placed water and books on the table next to him. Then made sure the accumulator battery had charge in it for the radio, and left for work. Alice positively loathed her job, and her boss even more so. She had had too sound an education to be employed in such a mundane job, but there was no choice, due to her responsibilities.

By the time she arrived at the office she had gathered her thoughts together. Having taken off her coat and scarf and straightened her skirt and blouse, Alice knocked on her boss's door. He was a rotund, self-satisfied man who always leered at Alice in a way that made her skin crawl.

'Good morning Mr. Jenkins. Is there a particular job for me or shall I just get on with the filing?'

'Good morning Miss. Rogers. Yes, will you please sort out and tidy this filing cabinet. It's a mess. Before you see to that get me a pot of tea. Then take my suit to the cleaners. Also on your return I want you to sort out the stationary cupboard, and make out a requisition list.'

'Yes sir. Have you remembered I must pop home at lunch time to attend to my father?'

'If you must, but you really do have to sort something out over this; you're away far too long. I don't pay you to be a nurse maid.'

'Mr Jenkins, you knew when you interviewed me I had responsibilities that I can do nothing about.'

'Yes my dear, but maybe we can come to an arrangement that will benefit us both. This afternoon I want you to accompany me on some business,' was his snide reply. With that Alice completed all the jobs Mr Jenkins had given her. She then made her way back to the flat to tend her father. He was in a very disgruntled mood. Picking fault with the food she gave him. The next thing was he knocked over his cup of tea. She thought *I'm sure he did that deliberately.* Grabbing a cloth she mopped it up. All the while she was doing this her father moaned and swore at her, telling her she could get a better job if she wanted to. He also accused her of giving him less food that she and her sister had, and what he had was just the left overs. Alice was in tears by the time she left for work. She was late, and knew there would be trouble.

Alice was trembling when on her return to work she got into Mr. Jenkins car. She tried to shut out his ruthless remarks on her lateness. Knowing it was no good trying to explain what had happened, she asked

'Where are we going? What is the business, Mr. Jenkins?'

'You'll see when we get there my dear; don't you worry.'

When Mr Jenkins brought his car to a stand still Alice looked around. All she could see was a block of flats. *What business could he possibly have here*, she thought. She didn't feel it her place to question his reason therefore she simply followed him into one of the flats.

What a shock she got when he instructed her to remove her coat. When she did so he lunged at her propelling her down onto the sofa. He dragged her clothes off. His hands groped her body. She gasped as the air was knocked out of her when his weight came down on her. She screamed at the extreme pain and horror as he forced himself into her. She knew he was perfectly able to resist all her struggles and scream's; in fact it seemed they added to his pleasure.

When it was all over, and he was sated, he gruffly told her he didn't want to see her ever again as he threw her coat at her.

'If you ever mention this to anyone I shall say you led me on, and it will be me, a respectable businessman, who will be believed,' he threatened her, and left the flat. The door closed in a final thud.

Alice lay there sobbing and heartbroken, beside herself with shock. She didn't know what to do. She felt nauseous and filthy, but was afraid to go home. She was sure her father would see something had happened to her. What on earth was she going to do now for money without a job? She was desperate. Feeling sore and stiff she found her ripped blouse and skirt. She pulled them on, and shakily managed to walk down the stairs and out of the building, feeling very self-conscious. She was sure that everyone who saw her knew what had occurred.

The enforced slow walk back to the flat was a painful one. Climbing the stairs, even more so. As she entered the flat her spirit dipped lower. Not only was she afraid of her father's reaction, but she also found the flat more depressing than usual. She had tried hard to make it have a homely appearance, but it just didn't. It was very dark. They could only afford a single low wattage bulb in the ceiling light. The floor had the original dark patterned lino, which no matter how often she washed it, it never seemed to look any cleaner. The fire grate needed a coat of blacking, but that was again something she couldn't afford to buy.

The prospect of ever having a decent life was non-existent. All this was made worse by her father's suspicions when she had to face him. She knew he could sense something was wrong. Alice quickly made him a cup of tea and excused herself to her bedroom before she dropped.

The next day Alice came out of the Labour Exchange feeling dejected. What was she going to do? She felt desperate. There were vacancies for jobs she could do with no problem, but her home circumstances stood in the way. It was so depressing. Panic was starting to set in. How could she look after her family?

She must be home each day to see to her father, and get lunch for him, or he would be even more morose than normal. Her route to the employment office took her down the main road past an appealing café. How she longed to treat herself to a cup of tea, and enjoy the warm atmosphere, but time and money prevented this. She had just reluctantly passed the inviting café window when she stopped short and went back to look at the notice in the window. She entered the café enjoying the delicious smell of food, the warmth and the hub of chatter; all of which contributed to its cosiness. With the notice in her hand she asked for the manager.

Mary the manager, liked what she saw in Alice, and offered her the job. The hours were only part-time, but fitted in with her duties at home. *Ah well,* thought Alice. *Its better than nothing. Perhaps something else will come up soon.*

A week later she started the part-time job as a waitress in a café. The money was so abysmal she struggled to keep body and soul together, but it helped that on the odd occasion she was given a bag of stale food to take home.

She was still worried as to how she would cope financially. To her revulsion she found herself considering prostitution in order to provide for her family.

Alice was experiencing difficulty trying to psych herself up to go on the streets. Then to her horror she realised she was pregnant. What on earth was she going to do now? Could many more bad things happen to her?

Her mind was in such turmoil that on her way home she did a very unusual thing and stopped off in the park. She found herself a tree stump to sit on, and did a lot of deep thinking. She had no one she could confide in. She felt absolutely desolate. After much soul searching as she sat in the park, she realised how much she loved the thought of bearing a new life. She frequently found herself caressing her stomach. Feeling a strong attachment to the baby within. She decided she couldn't abide the idea of an abortion, but what other choice had she?

In view of her pregnancy, Alice was grateful for any overtime. Julie was able to help with their father now she was older. So when Mary asked her to stay on that afternoon to deal with a delivery, and lock up afterwards, she was delighted to oblige. The delivery duly arrived. The deliveryman put the boxes in the back door ready for Alice to take down to the cellar. She tripped over her untied shoelace, and fell heavily down the last few concrete steps, as she was carrying down the last box.

Alice lay there winded and stunned for a few moments. She didn't know where she was. She eventually regained her senses. She struggled to her feet, feeling distinctly unsteady and in pain. She was sure she had twisted her ankle. Somehow she managed to pull on her coat. She locked up, and got herself home. Bruised and bleeding from cuts and feeling in a lot of pain she laid on her bed. Suddenly she had excruciating stomach cramps and felt a flow of liquid. Alice lay there floating in and out of consciousness.

Julie returned from school. She panicked at the sight of her sister, and rushed out to a telephone box to phone an ambulance. Julie wanted to accompany her sister to the hospital, but Alice shook her head saying:

'You must stay with father, he's upset and will be more so if he is left. Will you get his supper for me?'

'Of course I will. Please let me know how you get on if you can.'

After being examined by the doctor he held her hand saying,

'I'm very sorry, but you have lost your baby.'

'I thought I had,' Alice said and burst into tears.

'Is there anyone the nurse can phone for you?' asked the kindly doctor.

'No there isn't, my fathers disabled and my sister is too young,' she said between gulps of tears.

Her grief was immense. She had really begun to feel very maternal towards her child. It was a bitter blow. When she started to feel a bit stronger she had to make herself realise it was probably for the best. They already had a job to manage financially now, let alone with another mouth to feed, but every time she thought about it she had a few tears.

While recuperating, Alice was allowed to take her morning coffee outside. She found a lot of comfort sitting on the quiet lawns of the hospital. The sunrays filtered through the surrounding trees casting shadows. These she found convenient if it was too hot sitting in the sun. The lovely gentle surroundings were but a small solace for Alice's troubled mind. For the umpteenth time she longed for her mother, wishing she could talk to her. The nurses were very kind to her, knowing the circumstances surrounding her life, and the pregnancy. They gave her a lot of comfort, but it didn't stop her missing her mother. As she sat mourning the loss of her baby, contemplating her future, she was feeling desperate about how she could look after the family when a voice came from behind.

'Is there room for me on your bench?'

Alice spun round and saw a handsome young man standing there. She flustered and moved over to make room.

'Yes of course,' she answered trying to pull herself together.

'Thank you, I really needed to get some fresh air. Luckily, I'm going home in a few days. How about you?'

'No I have just been told I must stay in for another week or so, which has given me a problem,' she said, trying hard not to let the tears come. His face took on a concerned look.

'I thought you looked sad and pensive. Are you not happy here?' he asked in a gentle tone.

'I have a lot on my mind. I need to return home quickly,' was her cagey reply.

'May I know your name? Mine is Miles Granger.'

'I'm Alice Rogers.'

'You know a problem shared often helps to solve it. Would you like to tell me what is troubling you?' Miles asked.

Alice was very tempted. One look at him had told her he was to be trusted, but she didn't want to be disloyal to her family. Suddenly she lost control, and burst into tears. The whole story flooded out. Miles put his arms around her, wiping her tears away, and kissed her forehead. Her heart did a somersault. She quickly pulled away. She really mustn't get involved. Not under her circumstances. Muttering apologies Alice made to get up and leave.

'Alice,' he said gently catching her arm, 'don't go. Let me help you. I'm financially sound, and this may be a shock to you, but for me this is love at first sight. I have observed you from the passage window. Each time I've seen you I have had stronger and stronger feelings for you.'

At this declaration Alice was very flustered and hurried off to the sanctuary of her ward as quickly as she could. She made excuses to the nurses for the next few days as to why she didn't go out to the lawn for her coffee. There was no way she could ever meet Miles again. She was so ashamed of her life.

Miles was hurt at Alice's speedy departure, and her lack of appearance each morning. He hadn't meant to upset her, but he wanted to lighten her burden. She was such a lovely girl, and didn't deserve all these hardships. Her whole presence told him that her life now was not as she had originally been brought up. From things she had said about where she lived, Miles had a pretty good idea of where the flat was. When he got home he made a point of checking it out, and yes he had been right.

Julie was taken completely by surprise when she arrived home from school the next day. There was a box spilling over with luxurious food on their doorstep addressed to them. She heaved it upstairs and showed it to her father.

'Dad look at this,' she said, grinning from ear to ear in shear delight. Her stomach felt even emptier at the sight of the wares. She was puffed out with the effort of carrying it up the stairs. He was as surprised as Julie when he caught sight of her load.

'Bring it closer so I can see it properly girl.'

He rummaged through it. There was no sign as to where it had come from, but there was no doubt that it was addressed to them.

'We'll have a decent meal tonight, if nothing else,' Fred said feeling his stomach rumble at the thought of a really good dinner. 'Just make sure you cook it properly,' he said in his usual grumpy tone.

'Of course Dad don't worry about that.'

That night Julie wrote to Alice to tell her of their good fortune.

Receiving the letter Alice felt sure she knew the answer. How could she put a stop to this? She had no idea where Miles lived.

Two days later a nurse approached Alice to see if she would like to see a gentleman visitor, but Alice had no choice. Miles had quietly followed the nurse in, giving Alice no chance to refuse.

'Hello my dearest, how are you?' Miles said in an endearing tone.

'Miles what are you doing? I didn't say you could come and see me. You had no right to send all that food to my family. It's embarrassing.' Alice said feeling very uptight and emotional.

'Dearest, when you love someone as much as I love you, it gives you the right to do what you can to try and relieve some of their burdens. That's all I have done, but if you will let me I can do so much more. I would like you all to move into my comfortable home. It has a garden that your father would probably love to sit in. It's on the outskirts of the town in a tree-lined avenue. I could relieve the pressure on you girls by engaging a nurse for your father and purchasing a wheelchair to give him some independence. Please let me do this. I love you so much. Tell me, do you love me as much as I love you? Please say you do.'

Alice looked at him. She felt her heart lurch when she saw the love in his eyes and said, 'I do.'

Six months later these very words were repeated at what was their quiet, but joyful wedding.

Lightning Source UK Ltd.
Milton Keynes UK
UKOW05f1929181113

221353UK00001B/60/P

9 780957 447028